SHIFT OF THE WILD

SHIFTER LORDS

S.E. BABIN

OLIVERHEBERBOOKS

CHAPTER
One

My fingers and toes grew roots, reaching deep into the fertile soil, fortifying me, and in return, I pulsed nurturing magic back—the way of Earth, to give and to receive. Tulips and hellebore rose up through the ground, followed by bright yellow daffodils and lilacs. Vines dotted with lovely blue flowers curled around my arms and legs, and fragrant flowers sprouted throughout my hair.

I'd been on Rowan's property for a month now, and spring here was wildly different from the South. Where Texas might be in the 70s, Rowan's property was a brisk 52 degrees. I'd dressed in a cashmere hoodie and skinny jeans with thermal underwear underneath and a pair of fur-lined boots I'd removed earlier, and I still felt a little chilly. Temperature normally didn't affect me too much, but ever since I'd been here, I'd been experiencing odd fluctuations in power. Nothing too concerning, but I was much more sensitive to temperature changes than usual.

I'd forgotten how much I loved it here. Seattle was my original stomping grounds, and I'd done my best to put the place out of my mind after everything that happened with my divorce and attack in Scotland. Rowan lived about two hours away from Seat-

"

tle, closer to the national park and away from most of the hustle and bustle of a major city.

But if I wanted a little hustle and bustle, all I had to do was get in the car and drive a little bit to find some. Not that I ever wanted any of that, but knowing I could find some was nice. Rowan's territory stretched across Washington, Oregon, and parts of Idaho and Alaska, creeping a little into Canada, too. The same land happened to butt up against the territory I'd inadvertently claimed from Donovan. Even though the other Lords were still sniffing around, trying to find a way to wrest the Great Plains from me, they wouldn't be able to. They were Lords made by man and might. I was something entirely different—a steward of the earth. No one could claim the property I held unless I purposely let it go.

While I had zero desire to rule, I did have other plans for the land now that Caelan and I had severed our relationship. I thought about expanding his territory at one time, but after the events of a month ago, I'd never been so relieved I hadn't.

Trees rose in a crest behind me, the snow-capped tip of Mount Rainier peeking above the evergreens. Rowan's personal land spread for 1,500 acres and backed up to the national forest, ensuring the Lord would never have to deal with expansion on or near his lands. The place was preserved and pristine, the waters flowing cold and crystal clear. Wildlife of all kinds freely roamed, snakes and stunning birds, bears and deer, elk, cougars, coyotes, and foxes.

A few weeks ago, I had an encounter with a fox who stared at me curiously for a bit, then wandered over and curled up on my lap. Too hesitant to touch it, I cried a little at the beauty of the experience and questioned why he'd done it. Rowan told me he had an agreement with all the animals on his lands. He was happy to share, provided they never interfered with his pack or trespassed too close to the house.

I'd stared at him for a while, thinking he was shitting me, but when Rowan didn't crack a smile or elaborate, my thoughts had turned more contemplative. Few could talk to the animals, and none of them was a Lord.

A massive bear lumbered over and flopped down beside me with a moody huff. The first time he'd done it, I almost shit myself. Seeing a wolf in the wild was one thing. A shifter in wolf form was even larger. But seeing an 800-pound grizzly bear walking over to you all casual like was enough to make every muscle in my body tighten, and my brain to start flashing a danger alarm.

Grizzlies were already massive, but they tended to stop around five or six hundred pounds, unless you were in Alaska. Bear shifters, like wolves and swans, were much larger in their animal forms.

I buried my fingers in the soft ruff of his neck and scratched in the place I knew he liked. Rowan groaned and turned his head to allow me greater access. "Softie," I murmured.

Wicked claws scratched in the dirt as I hit his favorite spot. Unretractable claws, I found out later. Terrifying and hard on wooden floors, as I learned when Rowan in grizzly form snuck into the kitchen one night for the fresh-baked bread his grandmother had made, only for the poor woman to scream bloody murder and chase him outside with a broom.

His Keep was chaotic in a good way, full of warmth and love. Caelan held loyalty, but it was different from the loyalty Rowan held. I couldn't explain why or how, but I felt different here. Maybe it was the land, maybe it was the deepening friendship between us, but...I was almost jealous of what he'd built here. Caelan could learn some lessons from the younger Lord.

I lifted my hand and coaxed some vines to the surface, instructing them to cover Rowan's body. Once the massive bear was dotted with multicolored flowers, I whipped out my cell and took several pictures, laughing as Rowan gently swiped at my hand.

The sound of footsteps revealed Simone and Garrett, both who'd come at Rowan's invitation a couple of weeks ago. Thalia was somewhere inside, probably with her nose buried in a book or undertaking some kind of new crafting project she'd do for a week and discard until something else new and shiny caught her eye.

Simone snorted at the sight of Rowan covered in flowers, and Garrett rolled his eyes, though amusement sparkled in the amber depths. He tossed a cloth bag close to Rowan's head.

"Everything okay?" I asked as Simone lowered herself to sit beside me.

"Fine," she assured me. "We got a call a little while ago and wanted to talk to you."

Rowan shifted in a flash of light. I averted my eyes as he reached for the bag and hurriedly dressed.

"Moira has an idea," Garrett said slowly. "We wanted to see what you thought about it."

"And Rowan," Simone said. "Since her plan will directly affect his territory."

"I'm all ears," Rowan said as he sat back down beside me, dressed in a sweatshirt and an old pair of jeans. He tossed me an extra pair of wool socks and unfolded another pair for himself.

"Moira told us the situation in Joy Springs has become untenable," Garrett began.

Rowan stiffened, but I'd been waiting for this since the moment he'd taken me out of Joy Springs.

I swallowed hard and nodded. "Is she alright?"

Simone reached over and squeezed my hand. "She's fine. So are Ash and Tess. There haven't been any direct attacks, not with your mother and father keeping watch. But they're struggling to get supplies in, and the customer traffic has died down by seventy percent. Most who come in now are tourists, but it's not enough to sustain the business."

"He paid someone off to lose your shipments or refuse to do business with you." Rowan's voice was cold with fury.

"And the locals are afraid to anger him by patronizing my

shop. It was only a matter of time," I said sadly. "We all knew he wouldn't leave this alone. Caelan doesn't like losing."

Garrett's expression darkened. "He's playing dirty pool."

"Your shop is your dream," Rowan said quietly. "I—I can step in if you'd like."

I shot him a sad smile. As much as I longed for it to be forever, I'd been living and dreaming on borrowed time. "No. I knew I'd never be able to stay forever. Not only because of Caelan. I didn't even know him until last year. My Chimera heritage makes it difficult to stay in one place. The tattoos helped the power fluctuations but..." I trailed off.

Everyone's eyes drifted to my arm. My sweater covered the damaged tattoos, destroyed by Lugh in an effort to get me to shift and reveal myself. Hazel could have fixed them, but they were there to help me control my Chimera, something I'd already learned to do for the most part. In the past, I used the tattoos to suppress my other form because I was terrified.

Things were different now. After everything happened, everyone knew what I was by now, so there was no use suppressing anything anymore. Only a few people knew where I'd gone. I suspected Caelan knew exactly where I was. Rowan hadn't been circumspect in carrying me away from Joy Springs, but so far, no one had tried to destroy the peace I'd so desperately needed.

"You can fix them," Rowan said with a nod to the tattoo. "It would buy you more time in a new place."

Simone smiled sadly. "About that...Moira suggested moving the shop."

Rowan stilled. "Did she now."

"Her exact words were, 'The PNW is a nice place this time of year, and flowers are the universal love language'."

"She wants to move the shop to my territory," Rowan mused.

I blinked in surprise. Moira never had a problem with asking for exactly what she wanted. "Oh, Rowan. I'm sorry. I'll let her know—"

The Lord held up a hand. "Hold on. This is not something I haven't already thought of, but you will have to upend your life. And who knows if you'd want to stay here anyway. This territory is vastly different from where you came from."

Simone's lips twitched. We both knew Caelan had run a thorough background check on me. Knowing Rowan hadn't was refreshing.

"Not quite," I told him.

At Rowan's raised eyebrows, I laughed. "I'm from here. Sort of. As much as someone like me can be from anywhere in this realm. Well, not here exactly, but a couple of hours away."

Rowan stared at me for a long moment. "How did I not know someone of your power level was living in my territory?"

He didn't sound angry, more thoughtful than anything.

"Mom had her ways, but I was young and never made waves. Why would you have concerned yourself with a lone Floromancer?"

"I like to know everyone living in my territory," Rowan grumbled.

"I wasn't even in high school," I said with a laugh. "And don't tell me you know every single person living in the population of four states and part of another country. You're just upset you let me slip into Joy Springs."

Rowan pinned me with those hazel eyes. I never realized how much green his eyes held, and how they sometimes glittered like pieces of emerald. "I could have stopped much of your heartache."

My chest tightened. I opened my mouth to speak but snapped it shut when I couldn't find the words.

Garrett cleared his throat, shattering the moment. "It's not a bad idea if Rowan approves. His land has always been peaceful, and you'd be shielded by another Lord."

"I don't need a Lord's protection," I said automatically.

"No one said you do," Rowan said, still watching me. "Consider me an added shield in place. The Lords will hesitate to strike at you here, and so will anyone else. I've always been on good terms with the fae, even if I find your father to be mostly insufferable."

Garrett snorted.

Moving. I hadn't thought of moving back here since I left all those years ago. But the land called to my power. Every piece of earth called to me, but there was something about the PNW that made my soul feel rested. "You'd allow me to move into your territory?"

Rowan grinned. "Move back apparently. Since you were here once and I had no idea."

"Are there rules for shop owners?"

His brow furrowed. "Rules?"

"Turning over income to the Lords, background checks. Things like that?"

Rowan looked at Garrett. "What the fuck, man."

Garrett held his hands up. "I was in charge of security."

The Lord sighed. "No other rules besides what a normal city requires for the establishment of a new business. You do not have to tithe to me, Evie. I am not the church."

"Is there an open spot in the downtown area?"

"I'll have to check. Emberwood Falls does not often have openings come available, but I'm sure we could work something out if you want to stay."

Garrett and Simone rose. "Moira wants to visit soon. Call her back this evening. She has more to tell you." Simone touched my shoulder and nodded to Rowan before walking away, Garrett trailing behind her.

Rowan's gaze followed them. "Is it strange having Caelan's people with you?"

"They're sworn to me with a fae blood oath, so their loyalty is mine. But yes, it is odd having them by my side. Not too long ago, they were utterly loyal to Caelan. Sometimes I wonder if they itch to call and tell him everything."

Rowan smiled and lay back on the crisp grass. "What would

they tell him? That you've stopped crying over him and that you've become thoroughly infatuated with another handsome and intriguing Lord?"

I snorted and nudged him with my bare foot. "Are you serious about me staying?"

He rolled onto his side and plopped his head onto his hand. "Like I said before. You can stay forever if you'd like."

"I'm a lot of trouble."

His lips twitched. "You lived in Caelan's territory for years without a peep. None of us knew who you were. If I recall, it was your good deed that got the Lord interested." His eyes glittered. "Thinking back, I almost wonder if you should have let the self-righteous bastard die."

I tugged on the socks Rowan had given me. "You don't mean that. He's one of your closest friends."

Rowan said nothing for a long moment. "He treated you like you were shit on the bottom of his shoe. Your Lord moved another woman inside his Keep and claimed politics as a shield when you rightfully questioned him."

When I opened my mouth, he held up a hand. "Caelan's Keep has multiple buildings he could have housed that vicious bitch in. There are multiple ways to skirt the laws of good hospitality when it comes to the other Lords. If he wasn't smart enough to figure those out, especially when he had something as precious as you waiting, then that's on him." He sighed and flopped back down. "You still defend his egregious behavior. When will you realize how horrific his actions were? Caelan hounded you and wore you down, and yes, while I know your feelings were valid, how much of this was proximity and not giving you time to figure things out on your own?"

I could have said a million things. My feelings were real; I had no doubt. But there were times I questioned the speed of our relationship and wondered if we were a comet meant to burn out when our trajectory changed.

"Before you mention Lugh, I think you need to examine everything in further detail," Rowan drawled. "Yes, Lugh made Caelan see and hear things that weren't there, but the magic never would have worked if Caelan hadn't already had doubts."

I sighed and lay beside him, curled onto my side. "You make him sound like a villain," I murmured.

"Not a villain. Flawed. As we all are. But being flawed does not mean I would ever treat you that way."

"If I were yours," I clarified.

A pause, then a short nod. "If you were mine."

We lay there in a mutual quiet for a while longer before Rowan rose without a word, shifting into bear form with a flash of light and lumbered away.

I didn't bother waving. My mind was preoccupied with other things.

Caelan, my shop, and the potential of once more uprooting my life to move into another Lord's territory.

CHAPTER
Two

The video call revealed all three faces peering happily into the small screen when Moira answered. They were in the front part of the shop that hosted the coffee pot and small seating area.

"Evie!" Moira called, waving frantically. "We're so glad you called!"

Tess and Ash waved. I smiled and waved back, my heart cracking a little. I'd been gone for longer periods of time before, but never for something like this.

"I miss you all so much," I said.

Moira scoffed. "You can't start the conversation off like that! You end it being maudlin, not begin it!"

Ash reached for something below my view and hauled up a massive piece of pizza.

"New shop," Moira said. "They make amazing deep dish."

"Jealous!" Rowan's chef could cook just about anything, but he was formally trained and had turned up his nose at some of my requests. He'd made them, but I could tell he thought I had the palate of a rowdy toddler.

"So…" Moira began. "Did Simone tell you my idea?"

I nodded. "Yes, but have you told Ash and Tess?"

The vampire rolled her eyes. "Of course I did. They're both in."

I froze. "Seriously?" I breathed. Hope filled me at the thought. They were all willing to come to me if I decided not to return. The thought made a frozen piece of my heart crack open.

Ash and Tess nodded. "None of us is married or has any serious ties to anyone in the community. We've all been, for lack of a better term, lone wolves. If we hung out with anyone, it was with each other. You're family, Evie. And family sticks together."

I had to make sure they weren't doing this out of obligation. "Moira is sworn in as a member of my court, so she has to agree with me."

She snorted. "We both know that's not true, and you're way too nice to compel me to do anything."

True. The thought of making anyone do anything against their will made my stomach hurt. "You really do argue too much with your queen."

Moira crowed a laugh. "And you love throwing that title around when it suits you!"

We grinned at each other before my amusement faded. "We'll be leaving everything behind," I said quietly. "All the work we did for the business. All our customers. The friends we've made."

Moira raised a delicate eyebrow. "Friends?" she scoffed. "You mean the same friends who looked like they wanted to chase you down the road, wielding pitchforks and flaming torches?"

Ash grimaced. Tess shrugged. "We all knew it was both a possibility and eventually an inevitability," she said.

Moira glanced over her shoulder and shook her head. "Tess, you're being weirder than usual."

"My time in fae changed me," Tess said and stuck her tongue out at Moira's back when she turned to face the screen. "If someone can take me out of my life and make me forget every-thing important, then maybe nothing is important and we should live each day like it's the only one we get."

No one said anything for an uncomfortable amount of time.

"For what it's worth," I said, breaking the silence, "I am sorry for what happened to you. It was my fault and—"

Tess threw an olive at the screen. "It was not your fault. Lugh's the one who did it, and I'm glad you locked that scary bastard in monster world."

That was Tess' name for the place I'd stowed Lugh inside—a cold, gray realm made of stone and dirt, where monsters of legend roamed. He could no longer access any portals or use me or any other new World Trees that sprang up as bridges. Even if that world somehow grew a bridge tree, Lugh was locked to the land I'd thrown him in. His travel days were over, and I didn't feel a lick of remorse about what I'd done.

"It doesn't take away that Lugh was trying to get to me and used you to do so."

Tess's expression softened. "You can't blame yourself for the plans of a despot."

Moira blinked and turned again. "Who *are* you?"

I laid a hand over my heart. "It doesn't mean I'll ever stop thinking about what happened to you and wondering what I could have done to prevent it." I looked at all of my friends, my heart so full, and made a decision. "Go ahead and shut the shop down for now. Give me a week, and I'll make a decision. If we don't move here, maybe we'll go somewhere else. Somewhere with a fresh start. Tess, if you don't mind, can you strengthen the wards?"

She shook her head. "I would, but your mom and dad already made new wards. Caelan's shifters can't get within five feet of the store."

I winced. That was bound to go over like a lead balloon.

Moira set the phone on a stand and backed away, nudging Tess over with her hip. "Why wouldn't you just move home, back to the Seattle area? I know you loved it there."

I lifted a shoulder in a shrug. "I have complicated feelings about this place. And I don't know that I can lean on Rowan's hospitality. He's been wonderful, but I don't…" My voice trailed off.

Moira pointed at me. "Get those self-sabotaging thoughts right out of your head." She wiggled her index finger. "I can see them swirling around in your noggin. Rowan is so far removed from Caelan it isn't even funny. You won't be leaning on him for anything. That man would open up a vein for you."

Tears burned the backs of my eyes. "I don't want to be reliant on anyone ever again," I whispered.

Moira's expression darkened. "You never relied on anyone in the first place. You were the one who gathered us all. You were the one who kept us together. You were the one who started the shop. You were the one who survived everything and thrived." She leaned forward and her voice lowered. "Do not let that sono-fabitch trick you into thinking he was your savior. You saved yourself, Evie. And you saved us, too. We are here because we love you, not because we want to own you, and not because we feel like you owe us anything. Wherever you go, we will go. Like Ash said, that's what family does."

A tear slipped down my face. "I just need to know you want to come and that you don't feel obligated. If we do this, it will be a huge change for all of us. We'll have to work hard to get back to where we were."

Moira, Ash, and Tess looked at each other, then back at me. "We were getting bored here, anyway. Joy Springs is in the middle of nowhere, and Fredericksburg isn't our kind of vibe."

Tess and Ash both nodded.

My heart felt full for the first time in a long time. "I'll think about it," I said softly. "Until then, close up shop. You'll continue getting a paycheck and benefits. Think of this as an unplanned vacation."

"We don't mind working," Ash said. "There's no need—"

"How many customers have come in this week?" I interrupted.

Ash winced again. Tess nudged him.

"Four," he grumbled.

Shit. Much worse than expected. "Then it's settled. Right now, it's more expensive to be open than closed. A week, then I'll decide."

We talked a bit more, and I told them I loved them. When I hung up and set the phone on the nightstand, I let out a slow breath and sank back onto my pillows. Could I do it? Could I walk away from Caelan and the life that I'd built? Was it worth it?

A soft knock on the door jostled me from my thoughts. "Come in."

Rowan poked his head around the door and peered in. "Want to take a ride?"

My eyes narrowed. "Is that a euphemism?"

His eyes sparkled with amusement. "It wasn't, but it can be."

I laughed. "A ride where?"

"Get dressed," he said instead. "Wear comfortable shoes."

He winked and shut the door behind him, leaving me on the bed staring in confusion.

My bed was super comfortable, but my curiosity won out. With a groan, I rolled over and got out of bed to change clothes.

"I'VE NEVER BEEN HERE," I said, gaping at the bustling and thriving town square. It wasn't like Joy Springs, not at all. This place had a vibrancy similar to that of a larger city, but magic hummed in the air. "Are there any humans?"

"Plenty," Rowan said as he backed his truck into a reserved parking space. "But Emberwood doesn't hide. Every human who lives here is aware of us."

I snapped my attention to him. "How?" I breathed.

"Similar to your fae oath," he said simply. "If they want to live here, they must apply. Each human applicant undergoes a thorough background check, and a mage of my choosing performs an even deeper sweep. If they pass, they are informed of what our town holds and required to undergo an oath tied to their blood. They simply cannot tell anyone who has not taken the oath anything about us. The magic prevents them."

My misgivings must have shown on my face. Rowan smiled. "You wonder what happens if they ever want to leave."

I nodded. "Can they?"

His low chuckle wasn't amused. "I am not your other Lord, Evie. No one is held here against their will. They do not tithe or bow to me as a god. There is a simple spell that activates when they announce their intention to leave. Their memories remain, minus the magic."

I blinked. "How does that work?"

"I am not a mage," Rowan said, "but no one is harmed. They remember everyone they've met, but they do not remember anything of magic, only that of a fantastical city, one with whimsy and not power."

"You've never had a spell fail?"

"Once," Rowan said, his eyes dimming. "Before we could reach her, the woman's new city had dubbed her the kooky eccentric. Our mages visited her and made things right, but it was too late." A smile tipped his lips. "But she made the best of it and embraced her new status as the town kook. Last I heard, she was running a thriving incense shop somewhere close to Portland."

"No one gets weird about humans living here?"

He shook his head. "No, because our magic keeps us safe from harm. The humans know what we are and do not fear us."

"What a world that would be," I mused.

Rowan slid out of the truck and jogged over to open my door. "Come, Evie. Let me show you my world." He held out a hand. I slipped my hand in his and let him lead me toward the bustling heart of Rowan's city.

Three

ROWAN

She was here. With me. Her hand was inside mine, clutching my fingers tightly, with nerves or something else, I couldn't tell. She wasn't afraid. I'd smell it on her. Her heartbeat kicked up some when I took her hand. A good sign, maybe? I didn't dare to hope.

Those stunning eyes of hers took in the area, her lips parted in wonder. We were different from Joy Springs, much different. I did not lead through fear or intimidation, though there were times I had to remind people what I was made of. Caelan did not lead through fear outright, though he had a reputation for dispatching those who displeased him quickly and without prejudice.

I couldn't deny I'd done the same. Only a few times, but enough to keep me awake some nights.

There was so much I wanted, no, *needed* to show her. So many things I needed her to know. About me, my life, my people. All the things I wanted for myself and for her if she'd allow me to give them to her. But Evie was still wounded, still trying to find some way to return to her old life.

She had not realized that life had turned to ashes. Maybe she wouldn't realize it until she tried again.

And I knew the bastard would let her. Now that Lugh was gone, he'd realize how badly he'd been played. In some ways, he already had. He'd already removed Rachel, but I knew he would come for Evie soon. I'm surprised he hadn't done so already. Every day, I prepared for his arrival. Every day, I tried to show Evie the wonders of my land and my home. Every day, I resisted the urge to drop to my knees and beg her to stay.

She wasn't ready. And I was afraid I was running out of time.

Her fingers clenched around mine as I led her into the heart of Emberwood. Fairy lights were strung across the buildings, casting a warm, comforting glow across the area. A fountain burbled happily ahead, the water sparkling with fairy glitter. Evie gasped when she saw it and, without thinking, stepped ahead of me, tugging me forward.

I happily went along. No one had ever dared lead me before, but with Evie, I'd follow her wherever she decided to go. A few people passed by, their eyebrows slightly raised as they watched Evie tugging me along. Some of their lips tipped up in hesitant smiles when they saw me, allowing her to do so.

"This is amazing," Evie breathed. "Is that from the fae?" She pointed to the sparkles of light glittering inside and above the water.

Rowan nodded. "We have several sprites who live here. They charge the fountain once a week to keep it glowing like that."

"Cool." She reached her hand forward, then jerked it back.

"Go ahead," I encouraged.

Evie smiled and touched the water, filling her palm with the glittering liquid. She moved it to and fro in her palm before depositing it back into the pool. "This is amazing."

I let her explore as much as she wanted, reveling in the fact that she hadn't yet dropped my hand. She wandered over to a shop that sold stained glass. The owner, a small, sparkly-eyed woman named Leia, greeted me enthusiastically, eyeing Evie with interest when she saw our hands still clasped. Her eyebrows went up, and as Evie passed by her because her eye snagged a stunning floral piece, Leia mouthed, "She's gorgeous," and gave me two thumbs up.

I suppressed my grin and winked at Leia. Evie stopped before the piece and dropped my hand. I tried not to flinch from the lack of her warmth, but she turned to Leia. "This is stunning work," she breathed. "How much is it?"

Leia was not a cheap artist. Her work was worth the money, but her prices were sometimes eye-watering.

The piece itself was a beautiful work of art and oddly prophetic. A woman with long, dark hair blowing away from the side of her head like a ribbon unfurling in the wind, sat in a field of blooming flowers. Her back was bare, and one hand was tipped up holding a palm full of white blossoms, some spilling to the ground. Moonlight sparkled in the sky, a white glass ball surrounded by a deep blue glass background dotted with stars.

Leia's eyes narrowed. She stared at Evie for a long moment, then looked at me. "This piece is not for sale."

I blinked at the artist. I knew godsdamn well everything in this shop was for sale. Leia loved art, but she loved money even more. Evie's face fell, but after a moment, once she'd swallowed her disappointment, she nodded. "I understand. If I had something this beautiful, I wouldn't sell it either."

Evie smiled and drifted away, wandering through the store and stopping every few feet to admire another treasure, though I didn't miss how her gaze kept drifting back to the piece she coveted.

"Leia," I hissed in a barely audible whisper. "What the hell?"

Leia grinned, completely unrepentant. "Is this the Floromancer?"

"You know it is."

"She's beautiful."

"I know that," I snapped. "What's the deal with that not being for sale?"

She rolled her eyes. "It's not for sale because it's a wedding gift."

"A wedding gift? For whom?" I was supposed to know of any marriages happening in the area so the Keep could send a gift.

Leia's eyebrows rose. Her brown eyes sparkled as she waited for my brain to start working. And when it did, I snorted. "Today was the first day she held my hand. If you're planning on that, you might as well take that thing down and put it in a closet because it will be a long while before she's ready for that. If she ever is."

"But you were still holding hands," Leia whispered. "That means your beautiful Floromancer feels safe with you."

I glanced over to see Evie crouched, peering at something on a lower shelf.

"It is no small thing for a woman to feel safe with a male, Lord." She flicked her fingers at me. "Now go away and see if that girl will hold your hand again. You looked like a smitten teenager when you walked in here."

I snorted. "Mind your tongue, Leia." I pointed to the stained-glass piece Evie coveted. "And take that down before we leave, so Evie doesn't have to be sad when she walks past it again."

Leia put a hand over her heart. "Of course, Lord."

I knew I'd end up offering Leia three times what she was asking soon, and the succubus knew it, too.

I rolled my eyes at her impudence and headed toward Evie. She started to rise, and I held out a hand to help her. Evie smiled and took it, allowing me to curl her fingers into mine. We left that shop half an hour later with a promise from Leia to ship Evie's purchases back to the Keep tomorrow. Her bank account was lighter, but my heart was even more so.

I let her lead me through town for hours, and I didn't have to do a thing to make my people love her. She won them with her questions and her awe, and occasionally with her wallet. Tomorrow, the Keep would get an avalanche of packages, and Evie hadn't even gone clothes shopping yet, something we both knew she needed to do.

She'd come to me with the clothes on her back and nothing more. Moira had shipped a box of her things, but there was only about a week's worth of clothing. Most of the box was filled with books and chocolate, which had made Evie laugh at first, then cry.

I'd sent out my Omega, Hope, who purchased her a few more things, but there was very little of it that was in Evie's style, mostly joggers and long-sleeved shirts. And though she was thankful, Evie hadn't worn them at all until I'd pressed. The reason why had given me much pause and made me clean out my own closet.

She wore nothing made from synthetic fibers, except for the occasional elastane or spandex for stretch in athletic clothing, provided it was kept at five percent or lower of the total fabric content. The thought never crossed my mind. When I checked the tags on the clothing the Omega bought her, I realized most of it was made of polyester, acrylic, and nylon. Evie had smiled apologetically and offered to repay every cent, lamenting that she knew she needed to go shopping but couldn't bring herself to care too much.

I sent Hope back to the stores with all the purchases and had her try again, this time with cotton, silk, cashmere, linen, and sustainably sourced bamboo. When Evie saw the new pile on her bed, she came out of her room and yelled at me, then wrote me a check I promptly ripped up and threw away.

Yes, natural fibers were outrageously expensive, which seemed counterintuitive to the alternative of poisoning the planet, but they lasted for years. Plus, I didn't give a shit how much something cost. All the Lords were rich as Croesus, and I was no exception. I'd put her in furs if she wouldn't have my head over it.

I'd removed all the polyester, acrylic, and nylon from my wardrobe, kind of pissed at myself for never considering the environmental impact of my clothing before Evie. And when my new wardrobe came in, I had to resist the urge to pick Evie up and kiss her right on those glorious lips. Natural fibers were comfortable, breathable, and soft. Except for linen.

Fuck linen.

"There are a few clothing shops farther down if you want to look around."

Evie hesitated and shook her head. "I have plenty, thanks to you. Though I still want to smack you for that cashmere you bought."

I grinned. "But it's warm and cozy, isn't it?"

She gave me the side eye. "Yes. I love it."

Evie sounded so grumpy, I laughed.

"Are you hungry?" I asked. We hadn't shared a real meal since her arrival. The first two weeks, she barely came out of her room. The next week, I barely saw her inside the house as she'd spent most of her time exploring the property. Last week, I had to start sending trays to her room because her appetite was less than half of what it should be.

She paused and tilted her head to consider before nodding. "I am."

Thank the gods. "I know just the place."

Evie let me lead her to the best Italian restaurant in my territory.

And just like before, everyone who met her fell in love with her.

My hope was that one day, she'd see me as more than her friend. I never realized the true depth of my feelings for her until Moira called me, and I'd dropped everything to come to her aid. The moment I held her prone body in my arms, I knew the universe had played the greatest, most awful joke I'd ever been the victim of.

I'd somehow fallen in love with someone who belonged to another.

• • •

My phone rang later that night with a long-overdue video call. I thought about not answering so I could hold on to the high of the entire day, but I knew the asshole wouldn't give up.

"I expected you to call weeks ago," I said by way of greeting.

"She's there, isn't she?" Caelan snarled into the screen.

Interesting. Everyone in the square that night had seen me carrying Evie away, and yet he wasn't one hundred percent sure she was with me. Caelan had lost face with his people. Not good. "You look like shit," I answered.

His face was drawn and haggard, and his normally pristine hair was tousled and messy. The clean-shaven face he usually wore was darkened with at least two weeks' growth, and he wore a t-shirt with a rip in the neck. Caelan looked like he'd been on a months-long bender.

"Is. She. There."

"If she is?"

He bared his teeth. "Do not fuck with me, Rowan. Your actions are tantamount to war, and you know it!"

I couldn't help myself. I laughed. "We both know you're full of shit. Everyone knows Evie isn't your mate."

"She's my godsdamned fiancée!" The sound of wood snapping under his fingers was like a gunshot.

"No," I reminded him. "She's not that either."

Caelan closed his eyes, but not before I saw them flash with gold. He was more furious than I'd ever seen him.

"Is this how it will be?" Caelan asked quietly. "Have you finally stolen Evie from me? Is she warming your bed? We both know you've wanted her from the moment you laid eyes on her. Has your dream finally come true? Have you stabbed me in the back?"

I calmed my rising temper and drew on the one thing that had always saved me. Charm.

"That's a lot of questions at once, Caelan. Too many for this tiny brain to compute. Give me a moment, and I'll sort through them."

Caelan's nostrils flared.

"First, I've stolen nothing, not that Evie is a thing or up for stealing." I rolled my eyes. "No one is currently warming my bed, though I don't know what business that is of yours, and no one has stabbed you in the back other than yourself."

"Goddamn bears," Caelan said and sighed. His shoulders slumped. "Is she with you?" His voice cracked. "Just answer me. Please."

He'd find out soon anyway. "She is."

Caelan closed his eyes. "Is she okay?"

I lifted a shoulder in a shrug. "Good as one can be when the man they loved shattered their heart, I suppose."

"I could not help Lugh's influence," he snarled.

"You are so full of shit," I said with a laugh. "We both know magic like that only works because it relies on our own insecurities. Lugh played you like a violin, and you allowed it because you always doubted Evie." I leaned forward. "You brought this on yourself."

Caelan's jaw tightened. "Everyone has doubts in their relationships. It makes us human."

I scoffed. "That is an argument for a HUMAN, which we are not. We are shifters, but even more so, we are LORDS. You knew she was not your mate and chose to pursue her anyway. So aggressively, you frightened her. You asked her to marry you, then you allowed that wretched woman to move into the main area of your Keep."

"I was under a spell."

"A spell that would not have worked if you'd been sure of what you were doing. Fae magic, especially illusion and glamour do not work well on shifters, unless it has something to latch onto."

Caelan's face fell. "You do not think I am aware that I've fucked everything up?" he asked hoarsely.

"Not for the first time," I added, unable to resist rubbing salt into his wound. "I warned you multiple times. But this one…" I shook my head. "I don't think you can come back from this one."

"Do not tell me what I can and cannot do," he snapped. "We both know you want her."

"And if I do?" I said after a long moment of silence. I'd never admitted it, not the truth laid bare. Caelan suspected, and I'd screwed with him about it in a teasing manner, but things were different now.

"I fucking *knew* it," Caelan whispered.

"Unlike you, I don't plan to scare her into marrying me."

Caelan let out an annoyed breath. "I'd like to speak to her."

"Have you called her?"

His jaw tightened once more. "Yes."

"More than once?"

"Rowan. Stop being an asshole. She won't answer my texts or calls."

"Then perhaps you should heed her boundaries. Something you've never done before."

"Godsdammit, Rowan! Let me speak to her."

I smiled. "No."

"I will come there and settle this if I need to."

"This is not my battle. If you trespass onto my territory and attempt to harass my ward—"

"Your ward?" Caelan asked in disbelief. "You have got to be kidding me."

"Then I will make it my problem and expel you from my lands."

Caelan's eyes narrowed. "Are we no longer friends, then, Rowan? After all these years? Will you forsake me for her?"

I cared about Caelan. I really did. He'd been one of my best friends for years, but the way he'd treated Evie was egregious. "I never thought I'd see you treat someone so wonderful so terribly, Caelan. How can I be friends with someone who continually refuses to see how awful his behavior is? How much you wound her? You are not the same man you were a year ago, and I feel sorry for you."

Caelan's irises glowed with a ring of gold. "You presume to speak to me like that?"

"I do," I said sadly. "Come onto my lands at your own peril, Caelan."

I disconnected the call.

This would not be the end of Caelan's obsession with Evie. I could feel it in my bones.

CHAPTER
Four

I found the Lord in the kitchen the next morning, eating a bowl of oatmeal topped with blueberries and walnuts. He was still in his sleep clothes: a cotton t-shirt and flannel pants.

"You've changed your wardrobe," I mused, noting the comforting hum of cotton and bamboo. Every fabric hummed at a different frequency. Synthetic fibers jangled uncomfortably against my senses, though I was too polite to say anything. Ash was like me in that regard. The dryad always wore natural fibers, but it took Tess and Moira a while to fully understand how jarring they were to our senses. Tess had embraced the challenge and hit up every thrift store within a two-hour distance. Moira went on an online shopping spree and now grumbled about being spoiled by luxury cashmere and silk.

Rowan's brow furrowed for a moment before he looked down at himself. "Yes. I have a Floromancer staying at my home who made me feel guilty about microplastics and pollution."

I laughed and reached for a banana hanging on the fruit hook. "Mother Earth thanks you."

"Don't you want something more substantial?" he asked, frowning at the fruit.

He was always trying to feed me. I knew why. My weight loss was obvious now, the new clothes Rowan had bought hanging from my hips and shoulders. "My appetite is still up and down," I admitted as I settled beside him at the kitchen island. "I have a favor to ask, though, and it's a little personal."

He put his spoon down. "Ask away."

"Lugh destroyed my tattoos. They helped control the worst of my Chimera magic, and I've been struggling with keeping my power contained. I've siphoned some of my power, but this is not my land, so I'm careful about how much power I feed these grounds."

He studied me for a moment before saying, "You can feed as much power into the grounds as you like."

I smiled sadly. "No. I—"

"Whatever you tell me will remain between us, Evie. I promise."

"I accidentally claimed a portion of Caelan's land when I did that. When I return to Joy Springs, I'll have to rectify that."

He stilled. "You're returning?"

"I'm not sure." The indecision was tearing me up. If I decided to move, Caelan and I would be done. Forever. Was I ready to sever everything so completely? Not that he'd thought much of that when he stomped all over my heart. "Regardless of my decision, I'll have to return for my things and my plants. Plus, I'll have to relinquish the claim on my land to sell my house. Not to mention shutting down the shop."

"I'll help with whatever you decide to do."

Rowan had always been a stalwart friend, but these days, that friendship was skewing in a confusing direction. "Why are you always so kind to me?" I asked, dropping my gaze to study the banana a little too intently.

His soft laugh made my hands still. "That's a question asked by someone who has not had enough kindness in their life."

I frowned. "You've never made me mad."

He snorted. "Give it time. I didn't live in Joy Springs, so we didn't see each other enough to get annoyed."

"You've never hit on me either." Where the hell did that question come from? It's not like I wanted him to hit on me. Did I?

Rowan's eyes narrowed. He shifted his body to face me. "Would you like me to?" he asked quietly.

Um. No? Yes?

"You're an honorable man, Rowan," I said instead.

His eyes glimmered with amusement. "I do not try to take another male's female."

This was becoming a dangerous conversation. I no longer belonged to anyone. Not that I ever really had, but I understood his point. "When's the last time you had a girlfriend?"

Rowan blinked in surprise. "Curious about my love life, Evie?"

My cheeks heated. "I've never met any of your girlfriends."

He chuckled. "I haven't had a *girlfriend*, as you say, in a long time."

I took a bite of my banana and chewed for a while before saying, "Why? I'm sure you have women flocking to you. You're a Lord. You have all this stunning land. You're kind and funny. You look like that…" I fluttered my hand at him.

His eyebrows lifted. "Are you trying to say I'm handsome?" He crossed his hands under his chin and fluttered his eyelashes.

A snort escaped me. "Please. You know you are."

Rowan shifted and leaned in, so close I could smell the blueberries on his breath. "Perhaps I have not found the woman I'm meant to be with." He lifted his hand and brushed my hair behind my ear.

The light touch of his fingers sent goosebumps down my spine. I swallowed hard.

"Perhaps I've been waiting on someone," he continued, his fingers stroking through the bottom of my hair, lightly tugging the waves on the ends.

"Rowan."

"Hmm?"

I cleared my throat and sat up straighter. Rowan's fingers released my hair, and he leaned away, picking up his fork like nothing had happened, like he hadn't just stunned me into stupid silence. "Umm. If it's possible, could you take me to the border of Donovan's old land?"

Rowan speared a blueberry. "You mean *your* land now?"

If I had my way, that was about to change. "I suppose. I'd like you to come with me. If you don't mind."

"Today?"

"I know how busy the Lords are, so I don't need to go today. Whenever you are free is good."

Rowan smiled and scooped the last of the oatmeal. "You will find, soon enough, that I am not like the other Lords. I do not participate in all the infighting or politics. It makes me unpopular with the other Lords, but my people adore me." He winked to tell me he was mostly joking and rose to rinse his bowl. "Give me two hours, and we'll go. Sounds good?"

I nodded, surprised by his flexibility. "Sure. It's colder there, so bring a warm jacket."

He patted his flat stomach. "I'm a bear, darling. I'll keep you warm."

I waved him away with a laugh. "Incorrigible flirt."

Rowan winked and headed out of the room. I watched the play of muscles in his back until he turned the corner and disappeared.

"Get a grip," I muttered to myself. Pursuing Rowan was a bad idea for a million different reasons.

But the longer I was here, the harder it was to remember those reasons.

TRUE TO HIS WORD, Rowan was ready right at the two-hour mark and met me outside on the patio. I pushed a travel mug of coffee I made him over.

"For me?"

I held my travel mug up and waved it around.

"We'll take the truck. Got a jacket?"

I stood and picked up the one on the back of my chair.

"Good. Ready?"

I nodded and followed him over to the four-wheel drive. Snow covered the ground, crunching under the tires as Rowan pulled away. We're about five hours away from Coeur d'Alene, Idaho, a beautiful spot right at the border between Rowan and Donovan's —no, *my*—property.

"I put blankets in the back, assuming you'll need to be on the ground." He frowned and laughed at himself. "Which makes zero sense. You grow roots."

I smiled. "It's the thought that counts. But there's something else you should know."

He glanced at me. "Oh?"

"Sometimes, depending on how much power I expend, I do more than grow roots." I patted the bag I still held on my lap. "I brought extra clothes, just in case."

"It's in the thirties there right now and you're planning on getting naked?"

"Not on purpose. I might grow a barrier."

He blinked. "A barrier."

I explained what happened sometimes, ensuring he knew it was usually only when seriously wounded or trying to heal someone. "My magic is acting a little funny these days, and I haven't been siphoning as I should, so I'm not sure what to expect."

Rowan glanced at me again. "How long?"

I'd been knocking the edge of my power for a month now. The rest of it was building up inside me and felt like it was about to boil over like pasta water.

When I didn't answer, Rowan let out a soft exhalation. "Evie. You haven't released your power at all?"

"I'm not like you," I said quietly. "I'm not a true shifter. My Chimera and Floromancy are an odd mix, and now that the tattoo no longer works, I can't suppress my magic like I used to. I want you to see the land, but you can't be close to me once I release the magic."

"I'll be fine."

"Rowan."

"I'll be fine," he said again. "I'm not Caelan."

"I never said you were." I watched his fingers tighten on the steering wheel. "Is everything okay?"

"He called last night."

Shit. "Do I need to leave?"

Rowan scoffed. "No. Absolutely not. He wasn't even sure you were with me."

"But he knows now?"

Rowan nodded. "He was already ninety percent sure."

I didn't ask all the questions I was dying to ask. Caelan had tried to call me dozens of times, but I refused to answer.

"He looks like shit, but he's functional."

I barked a laugh. Rowan grinned.

"He insisted on speaking to you, but I told him no. He's obviously called you numerous times already."

I nodded. "He has."

"Thought so." His hands flexed on the steering wheel. "You don't have to speak to him ever again if you don't want to."

His words struck a chord deep within me. I'd been here for a month already and hadn't once picked up the phone to speak to Caelan. What was there to say? He told me I was flawed, broken, unfit to serve as his Lady. Some of those awful things came from Lugh's influence, I knew. But some of it hadn't. My father visited once with Rowan's permission and gave me a lesson in illusion magic, something I'd proven adept at. Dad said my talent was due to my Chimera magic. A Chimera was a creature made of pure magic. Since we could become anything we could set our minds to, why wouldn't we be good at the same sort of magic Lugh used to ruin my life?

But what he told me next stuck with me, burrowing deep into

my heart and mind, and I couldn't let go of it. Not sure I ever would, either. Dad told me Lugh's type of magic was more insidious than pure illusion and glamour. His power fed on our own insecurities, our own doubts and troubles. When I asked Dad what he meant, he smiled sadly, and it hit me then.

Caelan was struck so hard by Lugh's power because he was consumed by his own doubts about my womb and suitability, even though he'd repeatedly lied to my face about how he'd be proud to have me stand beside him.

His doubts did not make me angry. Those were normal things everyone experienced, human or not. Lying about it and saying all those awful things to me, embarrassing me in public, and making me feel all that suppressed anger toward me and himself...that was not something I was sure I could forgive. For the first time since he started his pursuit, he made me feel *less*. Worthless.

"Evie?"

I blinked. "Sorry."

"You don't have to forgive him," Rowan said as if he'd read my mind. "I wasn't there for all of it, but your father filled me in on some of the details."

I blinked away the tears. "Would you?"

He let out a heavy exhale. "Are you sure you want the truth?"

That was the good thing about Rowan. He never lied to me. Gilding the truth with gold didn't make it any less hurtful. I nodded.

"If someone I loved treated me the way Caelan treated you, I would assume that person never really loved me at all."

I sucked in a sharp gasp, but Rowan plowed on.

"If love has conditions, it's no better than a business arrangement. There are all kinds of love, Evie, but what happened with him is not a love mates have for one another."

Mate. Not the first time I'd heard the term, though it wasn't something Caelan and I had ever truly sat down and discussed. Not in the way we needed to. Not after this.

"When you are mates, you know each other's souls. You know

there is no doubt, no hesitation. You're both all in all the time." He smiled with a quick flash of teeth. "Being mates does not mean you won't fight with each other. Disagreements are normal, no matter what kind of relationship you're in. It also doesn't mean either one of you is perfect, but it does mean you're perfect for each other."

I studied him. "How do you know when you find your mate?"

Rowan said nothing for a while. "It's different for everyone. Sometimes it's like a bolt of lightning. Sometimes it takes a while for a bond to grow. Sometimes it doesn't happen until after intimacy. But every shifter can sense when a bond is building, though many try to deny it until it's too powerful."

"Why would anyone deny something that sounds so beautiful?"

He slid a glance my way. "Because men, no matter what species they are, happen to be idiots."

Our laughter breaks the building tension, but we're not even an hour into the drive, and I have more questions. "Why would Caelan want to marry me if we aren't mates?"

He took his time answering this, too. "I hesitate to speak for him. That's a question only he can answer. Not everyone is fortunate enough to find their mate. But he'd be a fool not to pursue you. You're powerful, beautiful, intelligent, and kind. You take no shit, fight for your friends and what's right, and you have a gift that makes the world a better place."

My cheeks heated at his words. "But he still thought I was flawed. He didn't think I would be a good leader to his people." I groaned and rubbed my face, hating that my voice sounded small.

"I have no dog in this fight," Rowan said, though fury vibrated in his voice. "You are the fae queen, Evie. You could have your pick of any man on the planet."

I snorted. "Charmer."

But his face was still serious. "It's true. You hold more power than any of the Lords, any non-human in the entire world right now."

I blinked, which made him huff a laugh. "Never thought of it that way, have you?"

"Shit. No. The queen thing came because Lugh was being a dick, and I needed help."

"Your father strong-armed you?"

I rolled my eyes. "Of course he did. We need to talk about that, too. If I stay here, he will have to visit. And Barrett, too. I still don't know a lot of what I need to rule a kingdom, and my training remains incomplete." I sighed. "Because people won't stop fucking with me."

Rowan grinned. "You're the fae queen, Evie. Your father does not need my permission to visit you. Barrett, on the other hand, will be required to check in. The Chimera are new to society, or at least to most of us."

"Thank you."

We fell silent for a while, and it was a companionable one. Snow started falling, a gentle wisp of flurries lightly coating the ground and road. Not enough to be dangerous, but Rowan reduced his speed a little anyway. "Does that mean you're seriously thinking about staying?" he asked later.

There were only a few cons and so many pros, so yes, I really was thinking about uprooting my life once more. "I have a lot to think about, but yes."

Rowan reached over and took my hand, lacing our fingers together. "I'm glad. You deserve to be happy. You deserve a fresh start. I know you can take care of yourself, but you'll have an added level of protection here. My territory is more densely populated than Caelan's. He has more open land and a larger area, but I have many more powerful paranormals here, and we defend our own."

"I'm not part of this place. Not yet. I never fully assimilated into Joy Springs. There were things I could never tell them, secrets I had to keep."

"Every citizen here knows what you are."

My jaw dropped. "*What?*" I stared at him, completely stunned.

"Is there a…newsletter or something? Gods, Rowan. You dropped a bomb on those poor people!"

"There is, in fact, a newsletter. Let me know if you want to be added."

I smacked his arm. Rowan laughed and smoothly changed lanes to exit onto another highway. "This was a meeting of the town reps. We had a vote."

"A vote," I echoed. "They willingly allowed a Chimera into your territory?"

"A Chimera who's been a model citizen and a business owner for almost a decade. A Chimera who defended another Lord's Keep. A Chimera who ripped territory from another Lord who failed in his leadership duties."

"You make me sound like a hero," I said with a laugh.

"A fae queen who stood up against a god and defeated him to save her home," Rowan said quietly.

Nothing he said was false, but he made me sound so noble. I wasn't sure how I felt about it. "You know I just wanted to be left alone, right? None of this would have happened if I'd stayed in my little corner of town."

Rowan barked a laugh. "Mess with the bull and you get the horns?"

I sent him a wry look. "Pretty much."

"If you decide to stay, maybe you can have a peaceful life once more."

I thought peace had passed me by the moment I decided to save a Shifter Lord's life. "Maybe." The thought was certainly nice, wasn't it?

WE STOPPED in a small town bordering Coeur d'Alene, a stunning city with views to die for. I needed complete privacy for what I was about to do, so Rowan pulled off onto a side road I hadn't even noticed until he was in motion and drove up a steep gravel road until the path ended.

I grabbed my pack, jacket, hat, and gloves and was about to open the door when Rowan popped up and let me out.

"Thanks." I slid out and hissed as the cold air hit me. "Shit. It's freezing here."

Rowan glanced at me with concern as he adjusted his pack around his neck. "You normally aren't so sensitive to temperature. Is everything alright?"

"I think it's the tattoo. Maybe it was helping me a lot more than I thought."

He helped me into my jacket and watched me put on my hat and gloves. Lips pressed tight, he looked away and up the steep and narrow path. "We have to head in about two miles. Will you be alright?"

I scoffed. "I can just shift into a bird and fly."

Rowan's lips twitched. "Forgot about that." He shrugged. "Or I could shift, and you can climb on my back."

"You want me to ride you?" I regretted the words as soon as I said them.

His eyes sparkled. "A red-blooded male will never say no to a good ride from a woman like you."

"Shut up," I said with a laugh. "You let me walk right into that!"

He laid a hand over his heart. "I would never be so crass."

I rolled my eyes. "Of course not."

"Whaddya say, Evie? Ever rode on the back of a grizzly?"

I shouldn't. I *really* shouldn't. But I was tired and heart-sore, and the magic leached into my bones, dragging me down. I needed to get it out and rest, in more ways than one.

He wiggled his eyebrows. "Live a little. I'm *very* warm."

Damn it. I was tempted. Too tempted.

"I can see that brain of yours working overtime," he chided, his eyes softening. "You're safe with me. We're still inside the boundaries of my territory, and I am its Lord. No one will harm you."

"I'm more worried about you dropping me," I grumbled, uncomfortable with his kindness.

He clicked his tongue. "Have you seen me? I'm positively massive."

"Arrogant ass," I muttered.

Rowan winked. "Climb onto my back, little wren. You won't regret it."

In a flash, Rowan shifted. A massive grizzly with laughing eyes plonked down onto the ground, waiting.

When I made no move to climb on his back, the enormous grizzly huffed and rolled its eyes, making me bark a laugh. "Fine," I grumbled. "But if you drop me, it's open season on bears."

He showed me his massive teeth and jerked his head, telling me to climb aboard.

What the hell. He was right. I should live a little. Who got to say they rode a grizzly and lived to tell the tale? I slipped off my gloves and climbed atop Rowan, something I never in a million years would have thought I'd do and held on while he adjusted, muscles rippling and contracting as he stood.

I gasped at how high above the ground I was. "Rowan. Do you want me to shift into wren form so I'm lighter? Or something else?"

He shook his enormous head back and forth.

"Are you sure?"

A nod.

"Alright then."

My spine was rigid, white-knuckled hands clenching fistfuls of surprisingly soft and silky fur. Rowan walked for a bit, then stopped abruptly and twisted his head, gently snapping at my thigh.

"What?"

He snapped again, then nudged me. "Do you want me to let go?"

A head shake.

I stared at him, dumbfounded. "I have no idea what you want me to do. Shift?"

Another head shake.

He snapped at me again.

"Oh. Relax?"

A sigh and a nod. *Yes.*

"Easier said than done," I grumbled.

Rowan leaned forward and settled his massive bulk on the ground once more.

"You…want me to lay down? On your back."

Another nod.

Dammit, Rowan. "Will you stop grumbling at me if I do?"

Nod.

"Fine."

Rowan lumbered to his feet and waited. I adjusted my position, finding it surprisingly easy because he was right. He *was* positively massive. Soon enough, I was curled onto my side, my hands still holding onto his fur.

Not long after that, my eyes began to drift closed, Rowan's gentle swaying motion lulling me into a much-needed rest.

CHAPTER
Five

ROWAN

E vie lay curled atop me, her fingers gently caressing me in her sleep. She'd be mortified if she knew. It wasn't her fault. I was very caressable.

I walked much slower than I should have, but she'd never trusted me quite this much, and I wanted to drag this out for as long as I could. She wasn't wearing a watch, and she'd left her phone in her backpack. Evie wouldn't know how long I took to get to the location.

Her warm breath rustled the fur on the back of my ruff. She wasn't a petite woman, but she was still small, her bones delicate and fine. The silk of her hair slid over me, swaying with every step I took.

We were making progress, but I wasn't fooling myself. Caelan would arrive soon enough. He wouldn't be able to resist drawing Evie back into his world.

And tearing her away from mine.

I wanted to fight, rage against that happening, but unlike Caelan, I would never trap her, never cage her, never force a choice on her she wasn't ready to make. If she came to me, she'd do it with her eyes and heart wide open.

Otherwise, she'd always harbor doubts and look at what those had done to her and Caelan.

She wasn't ready to hear all the things in my heart, nor was I ready to tell her. The beast in me had known long before the male. And I still wasn't sure what I thought of the truth burning like a supernova deep inside me.

Evie wasn't perfect. I wouldn't be in love with her if she was. She could be rash, prone to anger, sometimes vengeful when wronged, and furiously vicious when cornered, but none of those traits were flaws in my eyes. She'd been closer to death these last several months than she ever had, and she deserved peace.

Even her bastard father had said so during his secret visits.

I'd never had much contact with Evie's mother, but I knew they had a complicated relationship. Things seemed like they were thawing. I could only hope Cliona was not as hard on her as her father planned to be.

Evie shifted, her fingers sliding through my fur. She turned and slid her cheek against me, and it took everything I had not to shift and ask her to do that again, to my other form.

Get a grip.

I navigated a steeper area of the path, careful to keep balanced so Evie wouldn't slide off. We were almost to the area, close to the border of Donovan's old lands. She couldn't risk crossing over. Not while things were so up in the air with the other Lords, none of whom had contacted me since I carried Evie out of Joy Springs.

They were planning something. The bastards always were, but I couldn't find enough energy to care. If she ventured off my lands, I wouldn't be surprised if the other Lords, or Caelan himself, would be waiting there to snatch her up.

So we'd agreed to get as close to the border as we could, close enough so she could still access those other lands and siphon some of her ever-growing power away.

When she was done and we were back at the Keep, I'd continue showing her all the reasons she should stay here.

And stay with me.

. . .

Evie slept for two more hours, so long even I was surprised by it, but I did nothing other than lay on the ground and let her rest. She was safe and warm, and I gladly would have laid there for another five hours if it meant having her so close to me for a little longer.

She stirred, her face rubbing against my ruff. Evie gasped in surprise and stilled.

"Rowan?" Her voice was husky with sleep.

I tilted my head up.

"Are you okay?"

I nudged the gloved hand dangling off the side of my body.

"I am so sorry," she breathed, sliding down my side to the ground. Once she was a few feet away, I shifted.

Evie jerked her eyes away and waited for me to dress. Another thing to adore about her. She was uncomfortable around shifter nudity, though I'd heard the tales of her power drunk and glorious in her nakedness. Oh, to be a fly on the wall on that day.

"You were tired," I said simply.

"Yes, but you were stuck there for…"

"Not that long," I lied. I pulled on thermal underwear and jeans, followed by a warm flannel and gloves because I had no idea how long we'd be out here for.

When I finished, Evie pinned me with those stunning eyes. "You should have woken me up!"

"No," I said and grinned when she squawked in indignation.

From the pack I pulled two thin wool blankets and handed her one.

She took it with a nod of thanks. "You can't be close when I sink into my power. My magic is too volatile these days."

"Again, the answer is no."

When she opened her mouth to argue, I shook my head. "I'll be able to protect myself, and you won't hurt me anyway."

Evie blinked. "I—I wouldn't know if I would!" she protested.

"My Chimera form is volatile. I have a good hold on things, but—"

"You're scared."

She crossed her arms over her chest and glared at me. "Wouldn't you be?"

"No. Your magic is a part of you. I might turn into a bear, but I don't suddenly turn into a ravening beast and want to eat my friends."

An odd expression crossed her face.

"Do...you?" I ask hesitantly.

"Not anymore."

A surprised laugh cracked from me. "Explain."

She fidgeted, wrapping her fingers around each other. "When the Chimera magic was first burning through me, I tried to eat Hazel." Evie grimaced.

I pressed my lips together to keep from crowing with laughter. "I assume Hazel was just fine?"

Evie huffed. "She had one of those cattle prod things that shocked the shit out of you and knew how to use it."

I belly laughed.

A reluctant smile tugged on her lips. "I twitched for two weeks straight until I learned friends are not food."

I bent over, howling with laughter. Evie smacked me in the shoulder, but she was laughing, too. "It's not funny, you ass."

"It's hilarious," I said with a wheezing laugh. "Now I'm even more comfortable sitting close. You've obviously learned your lesson."

Her eyes narrowed. "Is there a shocker in that pack?"

I widened my eyes in mock innocence. "I would never."

She harrumphed and started looking for a spot to settle down. Snow covered the ground, so nowhere was ideal. We'd both have frozen asses when this was over.

Evie finally gave up and plopped right in the middle of the small clearing. "How deep is this snow, do you think?"

"We're higher up in elevation, and it's been colder than usual here." I searched around for a long stick and stuck it down into the snow. "About a foot," I said when I pulled it out and peered at the snow left clinging to the branch. "But the ground isn't frozen very far down."

Evie squinted at her gloves then up at me. "I should warn you about something."

I sat down beside her, about two feet away. "Still not going to move away."

"Sometimes when I go too deep..." She paused.

My eyebrows lifted.

"My clothes disintegrate."

I couldn't help the slow grin that crept onto my face. "In that case, I'm definitely not moving away."

Evie cracked a laugh and closed her eyes.

CHAPTER
Six

I began with a slow and even trickle of magic, gently breaking open the frozen ground to send my power spiraling through the earth. Rowan's comforting presence by my side made me feel safe, and I sank deeper, the first trickle of relief shivering down my spine.

Being on Rowan's land was wonderful, but my power itched to heal and claim. If I stayed on his property too long, his land would begin to change. At first, he might not mind, but he was a Lord, tied to his territory just the same as I was to mine. Having a Floromancer around might be great for the health of his plants, but Rowan had power similar to mine. His plants were already glossy and green inside his greenhouse.

Eventually, my Floromancy would itch to claim his land, just like what had happened on Caelan's land, and Donovan's land.

"I can hear your brain working overtime," Rowan murmured. "Everything okay?"

"Everything is fine. Mulling over some things about my power."

Rowan huffed a laugh. "You're worried about being on Keep land, aren't you?"

I cracked an eye open and looked at him. "Are you psychic or something?"

He laughed. "I can feel your magic. You're holding back because you're worried about claiming my land."

I gaped at him. "How could you possibly know that?"

"Donovan's land belongs to you now. A small part of Caelan's land answers to you, does it not?"

"I plan to give that back to him," I grumbled.

He inclined his head. "Then if you inadvertently claim mine, you can give it back to me as well."

I sighed. "I can't help it, you know. It's not something I do on purpose."

"I know," Rowan said. "You assume I am like Caelan or Donovan, but I am tied to my land the same way you are tied to yours. I can feel your magic, Evie. You're holding almost everything back. We're close enough to the border for you to let go of everything."

"And if I soak your land with too much power?"

He laughed softly. "You won't."

I frowned. "Why are you always so sure of everything? It's kind of annoying."

He scooted closer and reached for my hand. "Trust me, you grumpy little thing. Let go, Evie."

His touch was warm and comforting, the gentle hum of his power sliding over my palm. I closed my eyes and let out a long breath, allowing more power to slide from my skin. Siphoning would be easier if it wasn't so fucking cold outside, but having bare legs or arms right now seemed insane. Everywhere I touched the earth, I could release power from, but not when I was wearing clothes. Maybe I could bring a tent next time—

"Evie," Rowan grumbled. "Still your mind."

He was right. I sighed and went deeper. Something warm fell over my shoulders. A blanket. Rowan moved closer, his thigh pressing against mine. Gentle hands tugged my hat lower around my ears.

"Fussy nursemaid," I murmured.

"You're shivering."

I was. The blanket helped, but the cold was starting to seep through my clothing. "Because it's freezing."

Rowan dropped my hand and moved. I kept my eyes closed, trying to concentrate and doing a crap job of it, when warm arms wrapped around my waist, and Rowan pulled me back against his chest, his legs on either side of mine.

"Rowan." My heart pounded, my blood heating in my veins.

His breath was warm against my neck. "Warmer?"

I didn't want to say yes, but I'd already stopped shivering. Say what you want about shifters, but being cuddled by one, especially a bear, felt like snuggling up next to a cozy fireplace.

"Yes, but you're making it difficult to concentrate."

"Oh? How so?"

"Incorrigible brat," I muttered.

Rowan snorted.

"I'm worried I'm going to hurt you."

"Is that all you're worried about?"

No. He was warm and pressed against me and lean and hard in all the right places, and his breath was on my skin, and his hair was tickling my cheek and what in the actual hell was I thinking? A month ago, I was engaged and about to walk down the aisle with the man I thought I'd be with forever.

Now I was sitting in a remote area with my friend, my good friend, and I was *reacting*. He was warm and his arms were around me, and I was having trouble thinking about doing anything other than turning around and—

"Yes," I snapped.

He leaned closer, his breath warm against the shell of my ear. "Liar," he whispered.

"If you get stabbed with a tree limb, I'm not going to feel sorry for you."

"Mmm. Worth it."

"Stop being an ass, please."

He laughed. "Fine. But you are warmer, and you have a bear to thank for that. Did you know our body temperatures are over a hundred degrees?"

"Rowan, if I don't siphon this magic out, I'm going to self-combust. Please shut up."

His arms tightened just a hair. "Alright. Do your worst."

I sank into my power, Rowan's warmth helping my concentration, even though he was a menace. Deeper and deeper I went, reaching for Donovan's border, but more and more power spooled from my body, the normal well of magic far greater than it had ever been before. Even then, it had been immense, but now, with my tattoos damaged and my Chimera power right at the surface, I felt like a supernova burning with magic.

The ground, still slumbering in this unusual winter, responded, roots reaching toward me, gently wrapping around my thighs and waist, including Rowan in their seeking.

The Lord let out a soft gasp of surprise but made no move to jerk away or recoil. Instead, he pulled me closer until I could barely tell him or myself apart. Flowers bloomed around us, sprouting from my hair and skin, the land responding not only to me but to the Lord whose arms wrapped around me. Vines and roots and flower bulbs quested curiously toward him, my mind's eye watching as they gently nudged and explored the Lord's clothing and skin.

He is your Lord, I said to the land. *I am merely one of your stewards.*

The earth never spoke to me with words. Its sentience was profoundly different from humans or animals. Any communication came through images and feelings. And the land...it loved him. Images flew at me of Rowan in his greenhouse, of his careful stewardship of the grounds around the Keep, his choice of gardeners to help him with the things he didn't have time to do.

"The land loves you," I murmured.

Rowan's voice shook. "I—I had no idea your power felt like this."

I stilled. "You can sense what I sense? You feel the power below the ground?"

Pulling my senses back just a hair, I focused on Rowan. His heart pounded against my back, his breath ragged in my ear.

"I can. Evie, this—" He let out a long breath. "This power is staggering. Stunning. You—" He laid his head against the crook of my shoulder. "Are beautiful," he whispered. "You're the most beautiful thing I've ever seen."

My heart lurched. "Rowan."

"Don't say anything," he whispered. "I know things are complicated. But I wanted you to know."

All I could do was nod. My thoughts swirled, but the power in my blood was a siren song, and I sank back into the earth, unable to resist its call.

Gods. I was in such deep shit. Maybe I should have stayed in the car. I was wrapped around her, breathing in the sweet scent of her skin—jasmine and honey, rose and peony, a touch of my land's soil—ever changing but quintessentially Evie. She'd covered me in vines and blossoms, and if any of my wolves could see me now, they'd laugh themselves senseless, but how could I abandon her when she'd shared such a deep part of herself?

But the thing that both delighted and concerned me was how I could feel her power. Our magic wasn't the same; similar, but with fundamental differences. Even so, there was never a time when I felt the same things she felt or heard the land's call through my soul. Something was happening, something bigger than me or Evie. If I knew what was good for me, I'd unwrap myself from temptation and allow her to finish this without me.

I'd held her before, but never this intimately, and never had we melted into each other like this. I could *see* Evie, so deep inside her I felt myself falling into a massive abyss I knew I wouldn't be able to climb out of later. She was fundamentally good, something few people could claim. Evie's love was a never-ending well of emotion, one that if she ever gifted me with a tenth of that well, I'd never be able to walk away.

I thought I'd understood Caelan's obsession with her before, but I hadn't. Not until now. And I knew the sonofabitch hadn't felt even a smidge of what I was feeling right now, or if he'd ever accompanied her during one of these jaunts.

My breathing stayed steady and even, matching Evie's own breath patterns, even with my thoughts spiraling. To top all of this, Evie had just reacted to me. A non-shifter or a shifter without as powerful a nose as I had would never have known, but I could smell her desire when I'd held her tight and whispered against her skin. Her confusion over her feelings didn't overpower how she reacted to me.

Maybe there really was a chance.

Evie continued spiraling her power into the ground, turning once she reached a certain depth toward Donovan's old land. Her magic saturated everything around us, the soft susurrations of growing things, even after a snowstorm sliding over frozen ground.

Her pulse throbbed, and I resisted the urge to press a kiss to the smooth column of her neck, instead focusing on her power to ensure she didn't go too deep. She didn't ask me to do this for her, but I could feel how deep her magic went, even though I couldn't explain why. If she passed her threshold, there was a chance she'd lose control. Already concerned with some of the odd aftereffects of the damaged tattoo and concerned about harming me, Evie had started off being too careful.

But now, she no longer noticed me as her body relaxed, the nervous rigidity she held when I put my arms around her, had turned into pliant softness, her back slowly curving into my chest. As we sat together, her head drifted back, resting on my chest. Evie's hair lifted and swirled in a phantom wind as she siphoned excess power away, a soft watermelon tourmaline-colored sparkle spiraling around us.

I felt the moment she hit the other property, the sharp tang of

Donovan's Lord power fading under the gentle onslaught of her Floromancy. Eventually, when Evie spent more time on the land, Donovan's influence would fade completely—if she decided to keep the property. So far, she seemed like she wanted to wash her hands of the entire affair. Not to mention the other Lords still being pissed over what they considered a theft. My opinion, especially when it came to Evie, was simple.

Might makes right.

A low moan escaped from Evie's throat, a sound that tightened everything inside me. I loosened my grip and readjusted, but she hadn't moved. A small furrow formed between her brows, and I stilled. Closing my eyes, I concentrated, searching for any issues, when I felt it. Something on the border of my land is corrupting the ground, leaking dark magic into the ground.

The area is small, concentrated into an almost perfect square, maybe two feet by two feet. Evie moaned again, her heartbeat picking up in rhythm.

Something had gone terribly wrong.

Rowan was in danger, but the power I could usually control had gone rogue. A darkness had leached into the border between Donovan's old property and Rowan's. Guilt flooded me. I'd neglected the property. If I had visited more often, I could have caught this before whatever this was spread.

The spot itself wasn't large, only a couple of square feet, but the malevolence pulsing from it gave me pause. Rowan was with me, somehow entwined in my power, with me and not with me at the same time. Speech was useless, but I felt the sharpening of his awareness as my power probed the spot, seeking to understand first, then destroy.

I kept trying to pull back to no avail. Floromancy was meant to heal the earth and whatever this thing was seeping into the ground was anathema. Curious, my magic circled closer and closer, seeking to understand what was poisoning the land.

On the outside, Rowan's heartbeat galloped against my back, his breath ruffling the hair against my neck.

I tried to come back to myself, but the magic had me entangled in its grip, as if saying, no, I need you for this, and you must wait. Not being the master of my own fate raked at my soul, fury spiraling through my breast. Once more, I tugged, trying to spool my magic back into my body. I hadn't siphoned enough, but it would do, at least long enough for me to get back to Joy Springs and expel the rest on my property.

Evie.

I stilled, my magic sputtering as if it too were stunned by the voice in my head.

Rowan?

A pause. *I'm not sure how I'm doing this.*

Me neither, but I wasn't one to look a gift horse in the mouth.

I need you to let go of me. My magic isn't cooperating.

No.

Rowan! I'm serious. Stop being a…

Bear? Male who cares about you?

A stubborn ass!

I'm not letting go. In fact, I'm going to see if I can help.

Rowan. I'm not sure how we're communicating right now. I'm extremely freaked out and will examine it later, but right now, I'm about to go to battle with some dark sludge. You have a lot more to lose than I do. Let go of me and go back to the Keep. The last time I was trapped, it ended up being days. You can't be gone for that long.

Says who? Are you forgetting I'm Lord?

Godsdammit, Rowan. Let go!

Outside of this place, I felt him shift, twisting until he scooped me into his arms and settled me into his lap.

This is not the time for you to feel me up.

Amusement trickled through our bond. *I'm aware. If we need to take off running, I'm quicker than you, and this position will allow me to get up faster.*

No funny business.

I would never, he swore, his mental voice oozing charm. *I'm going to try something.*

My magic was still circling that black spot, but had pulled back some, curious about Rowan, too.

Outside, he linked our hands together, his calloused fingers scraping over my palms. A soft green light sank into the ground below our feet, its shape akin to roots.

Rowan. He was not what he said he was. Or not only what he said. Rowan was much more than he seemed.

But he was intently concentrating on that magic moving toward mine and said nothing until it stopped right next to my tourmaline-colored power.

Think we can merge them?

No idea, but I can try. I nudged my already questing power toward Rowan's. The moment mine touched Rowan's, the normal watermelon tourmaline color flashed a burnished gold, something I had never seen or felt it do before, and the two powers twisted together into something new, something that reminded me a bit of a DNA helix. Cool, wild magic rushed over my soul, the feeling unlike anything I'd ever experienced. Not bad, but different.

Should we be worried about this?

You're trapped underground due to misbehaving power. Let's worry about that before we worry about our magic melding. He paused. *Let's see if we can clear whatever this is before we don't have a choice.*

Ready? I was anything but.

Let's go.

As one we pushed toward that darkness, our melded power seeking straight toward the heart of the mass. At first, nothing happened, only a slight sense of resistance as we pushed through, both of us straining with the effort.

An oily sense of malevolence fell onto my shoulders, a wet, suffocating blanket of darkness blocking out everything good.

Rowan sucked in a breath. *Keep pushing,* he gritted.

Underneath us, the ground rumbled, snow shifting and sliding against our bodies outside. If we weren't careful, we'd end up under the snow. Not that being cold was our biggest worry at the current moment.

Our magic touched the heart of that darkness.

We plunged into absolute darkness.

I could handle many things and had. An absentee mother, a

terrible marriage, a violent assault, life-altering genetic changes, but darkness…this absolute nothingness made me go still. A tremor rolled down my spine at the absence of any light. Even our melded powers had snuffed out or disappeared, but they were gone. Everything was gone. It was only me, only me, and I was alone like I'd been alone so many times, and was this death? Had I died? Was I doomed to drift in this nothingness forever and ever? This eternal hell of sensory deprivation—

Evie.

I flailed, a scream tearing from my throat.

Evie.

Nothing could penetrate this blackness. I must have died and this was my karma.

The scream went on and on, and it would go on forever. Surely there must be something ahead, surely there wasn't only this. My breath came in short spurts, my heart pounded against my chest, but if there was nothing, then I was nothing. Wasn't I?

Heat touched my lips, firm and unyielding pressure. Something slid in my hair, then a firm grip against the back of my scalp, tilting my head back. Warmth. Comfort. Fingers ran over my jawline, down my collar and stopped at my throat.

Evie, Rowan whispered against my lips. *Come back to me.*

He kissed me again, more insistent, his tongue sliding against the seam of my mouth until I opened. Heat roared in my veins, his touch different but not unwelcome. His kiss was claiming, but tender. Outside, I turned toward him, running my hands up the tense cords of his neck, fingers roaming through the thick, shaggy mane of his hair. His hands dropped to my waist and pulled me closer, never breaking the contact of our kiss.

Slowly, I came back to myself, my power, my body. I trusted Rowan, more than I'd ever—

There you are, he murmured, breaking the contact, as if he'd somehow known I was about to have an internal freakout.

His hand slid up my back and into my hair once more. *Touch grounds us. I was losing you.*

My lips burned from the contact of his kiss, and my thoughts were an internal jumble.

We're still in the dark, Rowan murmured. *But I am with you. We can discuss what happened later if you like. For now, we are both outside and inside this place, whatever it is. Focus on only this, Evie.*

I let out a long breath. *Thank you.* My mental voice was more of a croak, but at least I could speak.

Amusement filled the link. *I'll never pass up the opportunity to kiss a beautiful woman, even in a life-or-death situation.*

Ass. But his words and touch had jarred me from my terror. We still floated in a sea of obsidian, but he was here with me.

I was not alone.

Do you feel anything?

Other than the weight of that oppressive darkness, no. Nothing here feels alive.

I agreed and reached for my magic. Even though I couldn't see it, it had not disappeared. Rowan's power still melded with mine.

Concentrating, I followed the threads of power, seeking into the heart of darkness.

There, Rowan said. *Can you feel it?*

Yes. We joined hands once more and plunged into a sea of obsidian night.

CHAPTER
Nine

The magic had contaminated more of the earth than I expected, but our power was slowly eradicating that dark spot, showers of green and pink and golden sparks flecking through the oily magic.

Do you have more to give? I asked Rowan.

In response, he opened himself, and I did the same.

Power bled from my body like a broken swimming pool, flooding the area with light. Rowan gripped me tightly, funneling and weaving his magic with my own. Slowly but surely, the darkness gave way to our power, breaking up the blackness one chip at a time.

We'd almost finished when a presence made itself known. Stifling, monstrous, omnipotent power saturated the area.

Rowan froze. *Evie?*

I feel it.

DAUGHTER AND SON OF MY WORLD, DARKNESS HAS COME TO THESE LANDS.

Holy fucking shit, Rowan whispered through the link.

My fingers tightened on his arm. *Mother Earth. Let me do the talking. Be subservient.*

I'm a bear.

As best you can if you don't want to get smashed into smithereens.

Mother Earth sounds kinda mean.

I CAN HEAR YOUR THOUGHTS IN THIS PLACE.

Oops.

What is this? I asked.

ONE OF MY SISTERS. SHE IS ANGRY AT YOUR ASCENSION.

Of course she is. Can you tell me which one?

THAT IS AGAINST THE RULES.

Rules? Rowan asked.

I elbowed him.

YES, CHILD. THERE ARE RULES TO OUR GAMES.

And no one ever breaks them?

ONLY IF THEY DON'T GET CAUGHT.

Will you get caught if you tell me who did this?

THEY ARE WATCHING.

Underground? Who is they?

Amusement sparkled in the air. CLEVER GIRL. REMEMBER MY WORDS. MY SISTERS ARE ANGRY. BEWARE THEIR FURY.

I don't understand why you're telling me this. I don't have a tenth of the power you do.

Surprise surrounded us, there and gone in a heartbeat. THE MAGIC IS DEADLY TO ME. MY SISTERS KNOW ME WELL.

They strike at me through you. I frowned. *Your sisters don't sound very nice.*

Are you sure they're striking at Evie?

YOU DOUBT ME, SON OF MY LANDS?

No, Rowan assured her. *But I prefer facts over opinion.*

I resisted the urge to pinch him for being sassy to Mother Earth.

PERHAPS THEY STRIKE AT BOTH OF US. SHE IS MY DAUGHTER AND IS TIED TO THE LAND AS MUCH AS ME OR YOU. BUT HER BLOOD IS PURE.

Pure? I echoed. *You cannot sense the otherness inside of me?*

She laughed, the sound not the gentle tinkling of bells one would think when dealing with an earth goddess. No, this was the booming sound of a hundred hurricanes, the shriek of tornadoes, and the howl of a thousand wolves.

While I was delighted to amuse Mother Earth, I hoped I'd never hear her laugh again.

WE ARE MORE THAN OUR BLOOD, DAUGHTER. YOU HAVE BEEN AN EXCELLENT STEWARD OF MY LAND, AND YOUR MAGIC HAS ONLY BENEFITED FROM YOUR MIXED BLOOD. YOUR BEAST IS NO CURSE, EVIE. IT IS A BLESSING, ONE THAT WILL BRING GREATNESS TO YOUR FUTURE LINE. PERHAPS ONE DAY YOU WILL SEE THAT.

The day that happened was probably far off. Accepting and learning my magic was all I had the mental capacity to do for now.

Maybe, I said because you didn't leave a goddess hanging.

I SEE THINGS, DAUGHTER. YOU WILL, TOO. SEE WHAT THEY DO TO OUR LANDS. SEE AND HEAL.

I don't know how. I'm one Floromancer. How many places like this are there?

YOU ARE *THE* FLOROMANCER. YOU ARE THE QUEEN OF OUR PEOPLE. THE FAE QUEEN DOES NOT DOUBT HER POWER.

A pause.

MY SON STANDS NEXT TO YOU WHEN THE OTHER YOU ONCE COVETED STAYS AWAY. THINK ON THIS, EVIE. YOUR MAGICS PLAY.

Rowan's amusement was palpable.

HE WILL HELP YOU. SEE, EVIE. SEE, ROWAN. SEE AND HEAL.

That undefinable, massive presence rolled over us. Pressure built inside my chest, right at the spot where—

Oh shit. Rowan. Hold on tight. Do NOT let go.

The Lord did not question the urgency in my voice, only tightened his grip and held on.

Mother Earth's thunderous laughter followed us as we hurtled through the universe.

CHAPTER

Ten

ROWAN

'd been with Evie for barely a month, and today, only the second day she'd ventured from the Keep, she was hurtling through the world after speaking to a freaking goddess.

I'd suspected already, but after today, I knew being with her would be a constant adventure. Sometimes, like today, those adventures might not be good for our health.

I held on tightly, wrapped around her like a grizzly bear backpack, as we flew through the universe or wherever we were. We floated in a sea of stars and galaxies, soft golden light swirling around Evie's chest. Experiencing this...my lungs felt tight inside my chest, and I gawked like a child seeing ice cream for breakfast. Being with her was amazing. Being with her while experiencing this was on a completely different level.

Evie cursed under her breath, her arms flung wide. Magic sparkled from her fingertips, and worlds upon worlds upon worlds opened at her touch.

"I'm trying to slow us down," she gritted.

"Anything I can do to help?"

"Just don't let go."

"Can't say I planned to."

Evie snorted.

Different worlds passed us by, images flashing with snapshots of fantastical places I never dreamed existed. Places where ice reigned, others with fire. Worlds of stone and gemstones, deadly and beautiful animals roaming grass plains dotted with flowers I'd never seen before. But they all had one thing in common.

"Evie."

"Kinda busy, Rowan," she barked.

"Look." I pointed toward the left side, even though every single image had the same thing going on.

Evie turned her head, frowning. Her eyes widened the second she spotted the same thing I had.

"That's what she wanted to show us," she said quietly. "How can I stop this?"

Darkness was spreading through every world Evie opened, small spots corrupting everything they touched. Where the magic rose, plants and animals died.

"The fae are born from the heart of the world. Their magic depends on how strong the universal heart beats," she said. "Who would poison something we're supposed to love?"

She opened more worlds, searching desperately for one uncorrupted by the power, but there were none to be found. All around us corruption seeped.

"If this is a spell, we can find a way to break it."

Evie sighed and leaned against me, her fingers moving to close the portals.

"Your magic is changing," I said, watching how fast she worked to close everything as we sped through the world.

"I'm a living bridge to the fae realms."

I hid my surprise, but Evie laughed. "After I destroyed the World Tree, the magic had to go somewhere. Instead of creating a seed to replant itself later, the damn thing decided I'd be a good substitute."

"Shit," I swore quietly. Evie had made no secret her time in the tree had changed her, but I hadn't realized the extent of her power. Or how much it might come to haunt her. "Can you get rid of it?"

All the portals closed, but Evie didn't pull away from me. Her scent floated up, tantalizing my senses. I wanted to turn her and pull her against me, but moving in this environment was too risky, and I wasn't sure she'd welcome the gesture.

We had yet to speak about our kiss, not that now was the right time. I'd done it to jar her out of her panic, not realizing how touching her might shake me to my core.

She shook her head. "I don't think so. Mom is hoping a seed will show up soon. Maybe if one does, my power will be absorbed into the seedling, where it should have been all along."

"You think she's right?"

Evie's chuckle held a dark edge. "Not a chance. Fate loves screwing with me. Give it a week and maybe I'll be able to grant wishes."

"Hmm," I teased. "That's a handy power. I can think of some things I'd wish for."

Evie laughed. "A harem of nubile women?"

I stifled my sigh. Her jokes were my fault. I'd teased her before about my dating life, and the other Lords had added onto my reputation because of my constantly single state, wrongly assuming I was a serial dater. I was anything but. Evie had only assumed what we'd all led her to believe.

And now I was paying the price.

"Evie?"

Her hands whipped up again. "Hold on. We're almost there."

Magic saturated our bodies as Evie opened another portal and steered us over. Seconds later, we were plummeting back into our bodies, the words I wanted to say replaced with a startled yelp at the abrupt drop.

Of course we didn't land back into our bodies. That would be far too easy. We were right back where we started, trapped underground.

"Did you mean to do this?" Rowan asked.

"Yes," I snapped. "I love it here, trapped underground."

The Lord chuckled. "Sorry. I just assumed we'd land back in our bodies."

"Again, fate adores me. It's a whole schtick we have going on. I do something normal, the universe intervenes and screws everything up."

Rowan, still holding onto me, laughed against my hair. "How do we get back up?"

"Technically, we're already there. This," I said, waving a hand at our bodies, "is similar to an astral projection." I sighed and laid my head back against his chest. "I'm exhausted, Rowan. I may not be able to get us back up there for a while."

"No problem," he said. "Want to take a nap?"

I really, really did.

"I'm serious." His voice rumbled against my back. "We don't have anywhere else to be. You're tired. I'm tired, though understandably less than you. Let's take a nap."

I thought about it. Until I was powered back up, we were stuck here. "Usually, I pass out after using too much magic. Today, I'm just tired. It's kind of nice, actually."

"Did you siphon enough?"

I flexed my magic and felt the pull of exhaustion but not a burnout. The well was still there, but it was almost empty. "I did." My eyes grew heavy. "A short nap. That's all. I promise."

"A short nap," he agreed.

"Mmm," I said and sank into Rowan.

I AWOKE in a cocoon of roses and thick and twisted bramble, the heady scent of roses tickling my nose. Something warm wrapped around me. I blinked the sleep away and shoved my hair out of my eyes.

A few things quickly became evident.

We were back in our bodies.

My clothes were gone.

The something warm wrapped around me was very male, very naked, and very Rowan.

I froze. Next time I did this, I was going in alone. If I kept waking up naked with men, I was going to get a reputation.

Rowan stirred, the heavy arm locked around my waist tightening for a moment. I knew the second he came to awareness.

"Evie?" his voice rumbled against my ear.

"Yes. Don't panic. We're safe. This is…somewhat normal."

"If this is normal, I'd like to do this every single day."

A surprised laugh bubbled from me. "Rogue."

He made no move to let go of me. "How long until this thing opens up?"

"Soon. There's no real way to tell."

"We're trapped in here?"

"Someone broke me out of here once, but I'd rather not damage the plants." I paused. "If that's okay with you."

"There's not a lot of room in here." He shifted and—

Whoa.

I cleared my throat. "I'm aware."

"So I can't really let go of you."

He could, but it would squish us into an even more uncomfortable position. "We might be able to shift a little."

"Where you're facing me?"

"Or away from each other."

Rowan said nothing for a long moment. "Is that what you want?"

"No," I said and sighed. "I think that would make it even more uncomfortable. At least this way, we can move a little bit. If we were back-to-back..."

His breath ruffled the hair on my neck. "Are you uncomfortable?"

I laughed. "You and I are trapped in a living cocoon, naked and spooning. Today has been weird all the way around."

"And we did other things," Rowan hedged.

Here we were. At the point where neither of us could walk away from a conversation we needed to have and, yet, it was the one conversation I didn't want to have. "We did."

Another silence, and then, "You are my friend," he said. "You will always be my friend. But...you're more than that to me. You always have been."

I felt the same way about him. "I know. We've always blurred the lines a little, haven't we?"

He exhaled, his breath warm against my neck. "What if we kept blurring those lines?"

I stilled, my thoughts a maelstrom, unsure of how to respond to such a...whatever this was. Proposal? Suggestion? Proposition?

I swallowed, my throat clicking. "You could have your pick of any woman in the world."

His voice dropped into a low, husky timbre. "I don't want any other woman in the world."

A slow glide of his hand over my abdomen, making every

muscle in my body tighten. He pressed a warm kiss to the base of my neck.

"Rowan." My neck tilted back, allowing him easier access, even as I wondered what in the hell I was doing. "I'm not the kind of woman who dates around."

"Good," he growled. Another warm kiss in the place where my shoulder met my neck.

My blood went thick and heavy, heating inside my veins. "That means I don't want to be with a man who does the same," I said breathlessly.

"Even better."

A surprised laugh escaped me. "Liar. Everyone talks about how much you date around town."

Rowan slid a possessive hand over my hip and gently squeezed. "They're lying."

"You said the same thing!"

"I lied, too." He dotted kisses all over, his hand caressing my thigh and up the curve of my waist.

A low moan clawed from my throat. Embarrassment heated my skin. "We should stop," I whispered.

"Why? Because you're enjoying yourself?"

I was. Too much. Way too much. I opened my mouth to deny him, but Rowan cut me off. "Don't lie to me, Evie. I can smell how much you want me."

"I'm not the kind of woman who will accept second place."

Rowan's wicked chuckle sent heat straight to my core. "I haven't dated anyone seriously in several years, Evie. I haven't dated at all in over a year. The well has been dry for a long, long time."

I froze, words and thoughts fleeing my mind.

"I've never been someone comfortable with sleeping around or flaunting my power with women." He took my ear between his teeth and gently nibbled.

I gasped and arched against him. Rowan's hand slipped between my thighs, the evidence of my desire causing a low groan of satisfaction to rumble from his throat. The sound made my fingers clench against his arm.

"Rowan, I—I don't know what to say. Why would you make me believe something like that?"

"The why doesn't matter. You were with Caelan almost from the moment you met him."

I shook my head. "No. I wasn't."

"Caelan staked a claim and warned us all away."

"You—you wanted me?" The thought floored me. We'd flirted, but I never thought someone like Rowan—

"From the moment I saw you, I wanted you. I know things are complicated, but I couldn't live with myself if I didn't take the opportunity to tell you." His clever fingers parted me, and the gods help me, I opened my thighs to give him better access.

His satisfied rumble echoed in the enclosed space, and he shifted, gently rolling me onto my back, his fingers still stroking me. The space was too small for him to move much, but he rolled onto his elbows, trapping me between the space of his arms as he hovered above me, those sparkling hazel eyes somber.

"Rowan, this is—"

His thumb swept over my clitoris and stayed there. My eyes rolled back in my head, my back arching. He dipped his head and took my breast into his mouth, sweeping his tongue over the tight nipple.

This was different. And wonderful. And frightening. And I wondered what in the hell I was doing but I knew I didn't want him to stop. *I* didn't want to stop. I reached for him, lifting his face to mine. His lips claimed mine in a searing kiss and something, a soft thread of light formed between us, sending a warm, golden glow throughout the cocoon. His eyes opened, a furrow between his brows as he saw the light, before something flickered in his hazel eyes, a deep understanding of something I wasn't quite grasping. He slid a hand down my body and gripped my calf, sliding my leg open and wide.

"Say yes," he whispered.

I ran my hands over his bare back, exploring the hard, lean muscle in his shoulders, before my fingers slid through his hair. Rowan closed his eyes, a deep, satisfied rumble sounding in his throat at my touch.

His hands played a symphony over my body as I explored him with my fingers, tracing down the cut of his jaw, the rough stubble of his five o'clock shadow scratching against my skin. Tears filled my eyes as something tugged deep inside me, an emotion that left me breathless with need and want, and the glow brightened inside the cocoon, a warm, burnished gold, the color of ancient coins and a summer sunset.

Rowan buried his face in my neck, teeth nibbling the sweep of my throat. He still held my shin pressed against the back of my thigh as he slid down to claim my breast once more.

"What's happening?" I whispered.

Rowan did something that drew a deep moan from my throat, those clever fingers sliding against the evidence of my need. "I want you more than I've ever wanted anything in my life," he murmured against my skin.

And even though it was reckless and impulsive and borderline insane, and my emotions were a jumbled wreck, something was happening between us, something bigger than me or him, and Caelan became a distant memory.

Not once had I felt this cherished, this loved. And I knew this wasn't love between us, not right now, or if it was, it was different than any other love I'd ever experienced, but it was something I couldn't explain.

This felt right. What had being careful gotten me? A bad marriage, an irreparable rift between Caelan and I, years of loneliness. I'd fled my home in fear for my life after being so careful for years to keep my secret. Here I was safe and warm, worshipped and desired. Here there was no judgment. And so, for the first time in many, many years, I abandoned all my doubts and fears, all my reservations about what could go wrong or what the future might hold, and I whispered, "Yes."

The word *yes* jangled in my skull, sending a splash of cold water over my libido. Evie was underneath me, splayed before me like a cornucopia, gorgeous and glowing under that light. Her eyes were closed, her fingers buried in my hair, and her lips were parted. Her heartbeat was a rapid staccato, her breath jagged as I worshipped her. The deep scent of her desire washed over me, straining my control to where I balanced right on the edge of an unforgivable act.

The warm and lovely glow coating our skin in a shimmer signified this act between us was not merely sex. It would never be just sex. If we continued, if I plunged between her thighs and took her like I wanted to, this act between us would be so much more.

I'd suspected for a while now, ever since I held her in her home and realized she was touch-starved. I was almost certain when I carried her out of Joy Springs and into my Keep. That link had threatened to spring between us several times, but Evie had not been ready. She was still so wounded and hurt from Caelan's betrayal. There was a part of her that still loved him, maybe always would.

This had happened because she finally ceded control, allowed herself to feel what could happen when she let herself go, and so had I, my usually iron-willed control shattering the second she'd moaned and arched her back into me, the desire I'd wanted from her for so long washing over me.

We couldn't consummate this. Not when Evie was unaware of what the act could mean.

But what I could do was give her release and try to ease her into something that had the potential to fundamentally alter her life.

If she allowed it to.

"Rowan?" Her eyes fluttered open, heat turning her cheeks pink.

I'd been lost in my thoughts for too long. Godsdammit.

She shifted, closing her thighs, and I knew she wanted to shift away from me, but she couldn't. Her face stilled into blankness and she cleared her throat.

"Evie, I—"

She shook her head. "No. It's fine. We—we shouldn't have done this anyway." Evie cleared her throat. "I'm sorry. I shouldn't—"

"Stop." My voice was an angry rumble. "We did nothing wrong." I moved to the side and gathered her against me, her body stiff and unyielding. "Evie."

"This was a mistake."

I closed my eyes and leaned my forehead against the back of her head, her silky hair sliding over my face. "Do you really believe that or are you just being awkward?"

Evie barked a laugh, making me smile against her hair.

"This does not have to be complicated. You're attracted to me. I'm attracted to you. We don't have to make it weird."

Evie paused, contemplating my words. "Why did you stop?" Her voice sounded small, and I wanted to curl up in the fetal position and die, knowing I had hurt her. "Was it me? Did I do something wrong?"

Anger flooded me. "No," I breathed. "Never. It wasn't you at all. Evie, there's something—"

A crack of sound shattered the intimacy, sunlight and freezing air flooding in from above as our shelter collapsed.

I threw my arm over my eyes to shield them from the light, but not before I saw the looming, smirking face of Evie's father.

"Well, well, well," The former Fae King drawled. "Look how cozy you two are."

CHAPTER
Thirteen

Of all the people to catch me naked and disheveled after a heavy make-out session, it had to be my damned father.

A slight warm breeze rolled over our skin as a heavy blanket appeared from thin air, draping itself over us.

"Thanks," I muttered. "Did you kill my roses?"

Dad rolled his eyes and snapped his fingers. "There. All better." The damaged cocoon repaired itself, the snapped brambles mending themselves.

"Yes, but you killed them first, and they had to experience it." I untangled myself from Rowan, sat up and ran my fingers over one of the pale pink roses. "Can I take some of these back to your Keep?" I asked.

"You can take whatever you want," Rowan rumbled.

My father held the Lord's eyes longer than necessary, a silent conversation passing between them. Dad's eyes narrowed for a second before a thoughtful look crossed his face. I don't think they were speaking mentally, but something had happened, something that made my father watch Rowan in a different way than normal.

Dad reached over and dropped the bag with our clothes

between us. "Get dressed. I'll transport everything back to your Keep. We need to talk."

Rowan dug his clothes out and turned his back to me. I did the same, and we were dressed in no time, every inch of exposed skin freezing in the harsh wind. A heavy jacket landed on my shoulders, and Rowan's earthy scent washed over me.

Something fundamental had changed between us. After today, he was not only my friend. Rowan was something more, something that sent a frisson of terror roaring through me when I tried to examine it.

I don't know why he stopped, though thank the gods he had, because if my dad had ripped off the top of our shelter when we were in the middle of that...

My cheeks went crimson at the thought. I would have self-combusted on the spot.

Dad's soft chuckle made me pick up a ball of snow and throw it at him. "Should I ground you?" he teased. "For making out with a boy when your parents weren't home."

"I'm going to murder you if you don't shut up," I said through gritted teeth.

Dad gasped. "Regicide?" He laid a hand over his heart. "My own daughter."

I laughed. "Shut up. And it wouldn't be regicide. It would be patricide. You're no longer a king."

His eyes widened with mock hurt. "Yes, because my murderous daughter took my throne."

"If I recall, your murderous daughter didn't want your throne. The current king twisted her arm."

"Semantics."

I rolled my eyes and finished tying my boots. Rowan was already standing, eyeing my father suspiciously. Even stranger, my father was ignoring him. Dear ol' dad had shown up *very* conveniently.

Frowning, I rose and gathered the blankets up, neatly folding them to tuck under my arm. "There's a truck some ways back," Rowan said. "I'd appreciate it if you took that back with us."

Dad inclined his head. "Certainly. Evie, gather the flowers you want to take, so we can make a hasty exit. What I have to say will not wait."

I snipped a few of the stems away and tucked them into the jacket pocket. A quick sweep of the area revealed nothing we'd forgotten.

I nodded to Dad.

"Join hands with the Lord."

Not Rowan or your Lord. Just *the* Lord. Was Dad being pissy for a reason or was he just having a bad day? I opened my mouth to ask, but magic swept me away before I had the chance.

I swayed on my feet when we landed right in front of Rowan's main home. "A little warning next time would be nice," I croaked.

"Evie, go on inside. I need to speak to Rowan for a moment."

My eyes narrowed, and I looked at Rowan, who nodded once. "I'll follow you in a minute."

His lack of concern made me feel a little better, but not by much.

I pointed at Dad. "Be nice to him."

Dad laughed. "You know, you never said that to me when it concerned Caelan."

I crossed my arms. "Caelan usually had it coming," I grumbled before turning to head inside.

The way those two were glaring at each other made me think they knew each other better than they pretended. I tried peeking through the door curtain once I was inside, but Dad was staring right at me and threw up an opaque barrier.

Just in case I could lip read, I guess.

Deciding to worry about them later, I carried the roses out to Rowan's greenhouse. He had a few empty beds he set up for me after my arrival, and I'd only planted a few things inside. The temperature was still cold enough for them to do well, and I anticipated being here for at least another week or two so I could help get them settled before Rowan took over.

That thought pained me more than I expected. I couldn't very well continue living in his house. Caelan and I had damn near been married, and we still lived apart. The thought of leaving my land in Joy Springs hurt, but home was wherever a Floromancer landed, and this area had always sung to my natural soul.

Joy Springs was a pretty place, but the spring and summer greenery tended toward scrubby rather than lush, and the summers could be unseasonably warm if the weather mages didn't step in. Rowan's land settled the restless pieces of my soul.

He wanted me here. Or at least he had before our make-out session in the cocoon had gotten so out of hand. With him being so weird now, had he changed his mind?

I blew out a breath and shook the thoughts away. No reason to let my anxiety spiral into full-blown paranoia. We'd never kissed before today, and that kiss had turned into something far deeper. I rubbed the place in my chest where that light had penetrated through. The warmth was still there, and I could swear I still felt a piece of Rowan.

"Paranoia will get you nowhere," I said in a little sing-song voice as I sat down on the edge of the garden beds. The temperature here was cool but warm and humid enough to keep everything alive. Rowan had installed heaters inside, but the roses would do better if there were a few nights of frigid temperatures. I'd boost everything up before I left this evening so no harm would come to any of his plants if he didn't turn them on.

My magic was almost back to normal levels again, the nap I'd taken doing much to restore me. I had a while before I needed to siphon again, but working in here today would keep that at bay a little longer.

With a smile, I gently extricated the roses, my heart tugging a little at the reminder of just a little while before when Rowan told me I was the most beautiful thing he'd ever seen. I'd never be able to look at these and forget what had almost happened between us. Once I'd situated the roses in the ground, I closed my eyes and got to work.

Fourteen

ROWAN

"Are you mad?" Cernunnos seethed. "She does not know what you two almost did today!"

Evie's father was furious, far angrier than I'd ever seen him, and I could recall at least two other instances where I thought he might murder Caelan. I had to tread carefully.

"Are we not going to speak about the fact that you were spying on us?"

Cernunnos blinked. "What."

My eyebrows went up. "How could you have possibly known what was going on if you weren't watching us?"

Cernunnos turned away and gagged. "Aaagh! Gods above, man! No!" He scrubbed a hand over his face. "I am a lot of things, but she is my daughter!"

I crossed my arms over my chest and waited. "Then an explanation would be nice."

He glared at me, nostrils flaring, before he let out a long sigh. "Danu rarely rises. When she does, our kind pays attention."

"Danu is Mother Earth?"

"Never say that out loud." Cernunnos rolled his eyes. "If she had her way, she'd destroy all the trinkets that have her painted blue and green with the earth in her stomach. She is far too vain for those." But he saw through my tactic of changing the subject and waggled his finger in front of my face. "I arrived a few minutes after you and Evie awoke and did not want to… interrupt."

My god. I was a grizzly for crying out loud, but even I was horrified at what he must have heard.

Cernunnos held a hand up. "I left for a little while because I assumed you were intelligent enough to stop what was happening in its tracks."

"I was," I snapped.

"Barely. And you hurt her in the process." He poked a gnarled finger into my chest. "When will you Lords stop hurting my daughter? I am patient because she asks me to be, but you are both walking a very fine line between life and dust."

I spread my hands out. "I have no intention of hurting her and today was…regrettable."

One of his eyebrows went up, rage making his eyes flare green and gold.

"Regrettable," I hurried to say, "in that I had not had the chance to tell her what was happening between us to give her the time to accept or reject the gift."

"If you had, what do you think her answer would be?"

I shook my head. "I think she would tell me no."

Sympathy flashed in the old god's eyes, there and gone so fast I thought I might have imagined it. "I agree," he said quietly.

We fell silent before I admitted, "I'm floundering. She's everything I ever wanted, and I feel like I'm fucking this up. Today was…" My voice trailed off and I raised my face to the sky. "Beyond anything I've ever experienced. She heals my land and my people. She heals me."

Cernunnos stayed silent, only studying me with his wise and terrible visage. He jerked his head and walked toward the back of my property. "You've asked her to stay," he said after a moment.

"I did."

"Caelan grows bitter and angrier than before. You will not

escape him for much longer. If you are to convince her, it has to be soon. Do not let him wrap her in the false cocoon of safety he offers."

"He knows she can protect herself."

The god tilted his head. "He merely buys time. If he had his way, Evie would stay at the Keep and become his Lady, there to lead his people, and stay silent in all other matters."

Caelan was my friend, but I saw his flaws when others might not. The god was not wrong, though I hoped Caelan would realize he could never trap Evie in such a way that she would not fight her way to escape. He was not an evil man, only flawed, and used to getting his way.

All the Lords, me included, were used to being obeyed. Our commands were law, but Evie had never been our subject, not even when she was supposed to be. Even before she was the fae queen, she was resistant to our authority and chose to keep her head down rather than get tangled up in a world that might expose her.

Look what happened when she did. She'd almost died multiple times. A relentless wolf pursued her, won her, then betrayed her causing her to flee from her lands, and then she made out with a grizzly bear with a wild crush on her only to get soundly rejected, and now that grizzly was outside fighting with her father.

Gods. This sounded like a terrible sitcom.

"You do not approve of Caelan as a son-in-law?"

Cernunnos let out a derisive snort. "Evie should marry a king, but those are in short supply." He stopped at the edge of a small pond and sat down in a cross-legged position. I did the same, keeping a safe distance between us.

He smirked. "I can find you anywhere, you know."

"Yes," I said dryly. "You've more than proven so today."

Cernunnos' smile held an edge. "My daughter will not marry a king, so the person she chooses must emulate the qualities of one."

There was so much I wanted to say, but Cernunnos was still eons more powerful than me. "You know what we are to each other."

"No. I know what you are to her. Evie is not familiar enough with our ways or the ways of the shifter to realize what almost happened today."

"You would take her from me?"

The god picked up a rock and skimmed the stone over the surface of the glittering water. "Unlike humans or Lords, I do not take anything from Evie. Too many people have already taken too many things from her. She will do as she pleases. I may guide, even manipulate her if I deem it necessary, but if my daughter chooses to leave you, it will be of her own volition."

A cold comfort, that. Reality was already forcing its way back into our lives. Corruption grew on my lands, and we lived on borrowed time until Caelan arrived. I bowed my head.

"I want her to stay."

"I'm well aware of how you feel about her, Rowan."

"Do you have any advice for me?"

I thought he might mock me, but instead, Cernunnos uncrossed his legs and spread them out, then leaned back on his palms. He tipped his face up, watching with glowing eyes as brilliant oranges and purples streaked the sky, and laughed. "I loved Cliona once, back when I was a stupid boy. If someone like me could ever be considered a boy. Even worse, she loved me back. We were fools for each other."

He never spoke about Evie's mother. She'd be green with jealousy if she overheard our conversation. "What happened?"

"I was the king of our people—a target for every sniveling wretch who sought power. Loving someone makes them a target as well, and Cliona, she is a different kind of fae. Her banshees are not well understood, and many fae fear them." He paused. "As they should."

His eyes met mine. "Loving someone means sacrifice every single day. Loving Cliona was easy, but I was selfish. She was the one who made me realize our relationship could harm the most important thing in our lives and our world."

"Evie."

He nodded. "Evie. Because we loved each other so much, but loved our daughter more, we agreed to become enemies. Cliona spent too many years shunning her daughter for her own safety. It changed her." Sadness flickered in his ancient gaze before he looked away. "And it changed us."

"Do you still love her?"

A ghost of a smile. "I will love her until the wind fades away and the oceans turn to salt pillars. But Cliona no longer looks at me the same. She believes I was the king and I should have fought harder for them, fought to stay with them, and protected Evie more than I did."

"What do you think?"

"Cliona was right, and I will spend the rest of my wretched, immortal life trying to make it up to her."

His words sank deep into my heart. "I will fight for her."

A single sharp nod. "I know, but you still keep secrets from Evie. My daughter has had too many secrets in her life. You will lose her if you continue to hide the truths hidden in your heart. If she is what you think she is, you must trust her, no matter where her heart leads her."

"Even if it leads her away from me?"

In an instant he was by my side, so fast I would have had no hope if he planned to attack me. Instead of violence, Cernunnos clapped me on the shoulder and rose. "Again, young Lord, if she is who you believe she is, the road, no matter how treacherous and long, will always lead back to you."

The god rose and held his hand out, a peace offering. For now. I took it and rose, Cernunnos' immense strength turning my movement into more of a soft leap. "Come. We must speak of darker things than love."

CHAPTER
Fifteen

A gentle nudge on my shoulder dragged me out of a deep sleep. My eyes opened to see Rowan peering down at me.

"You alright?" he asked, amusement sparkling in the hazel depths of his eyes.

My right hand was buried a foot deep in the garden bed's soil, the roses I'd planted in full spring bloom. The intoxicating scent drifted around us. I smiled lazily. "Sorry. I was more tired than I thought."

"It's alright." He helped me up and waited for me to brush the soil away. "Your father is waiting for us outside. Ready to talk, or do you want me to send him away?"

The image of Rowan sending a god away made me smile. "He'll just come back. Better to do it now and get it over with."

He inclined his head in acknowledgment. "Lunch will arrive soon."

My stomach chose that timely moment to growl. Loudly.

"I'm glad you agree," he said with a chuckle. Rowan held the greenhouse door open and gestured for me to go first.

Dad was sitting at a large iron patio table, his posture careless and almost human. If they didn't know him,

93

someone might think him a senator's son, or an entitled trust-fund kid. He looked younger than usual, his golden skin gleaming with immortality. His antlers were gone, hidden wherever they went when Dad was trying to appear normal, leaving a mop of sandy-colored hair mussed artfully about his head. It was only when he looked at you that you knew the person behind those ancient, swirling eyes was no person at all.

"You're staring at me as if you're performing a dissection," he observed.

I flopped into a seat. "Just wondering when I'll start to look like you."

His brow furrowed in confusion. "You look more like your mother than me."

"Not physically," I said, helping myself to the strawberry lemonade someone had left in a pitcher in the middle of the table. "I would like to learn how to adopt the ancient, menacing, violent vibe you have going on, though."

Dad frowned and looked down at his casual attire. "I thought this was the outfit of an easygoing American male."

Rowan, who'd taken up the seat next to me, pressed his lips together and looked down at the table.

"It is," I assured him. "But you are not the average American male, nor are you easygoing. We can try to shove ourselves into a box, but we aren't box-shaped."

"Hmm," Dad said to himself, as if I'd given him a vexing problem to solve.

A slight woman came out, carrying a large wooden board filled with crackers, meats, cheeses, various jams, and different types of honey. "Something to tide you over before the main course is served." She set it in the middle of the table, dipped her head to Rowan, and turned without waiting for a response.

Rowan handed me and Dad a plate. "Please, Evie. You haven't eaten anything since we've been home."

You didn't have to tell me twice. Once I'd served myself a

heaping plate, I dug in. Rowan and Dad did as well, and we fell silent for a while as we ate.

Once the main course was served, a traditional beef stroganoff with mashed potatoes, Dad took a sip of his water and cleared his throat.

"I know you met Danu earlier."

"Technically, no," I said. "She never appeared, only spoke to us, then shoved us out of the dirt and into the universe."

"Sounds like something she'd do," Dad grumbled.

"Is she hideous? Is that why she didn't show her face?" I grinned at Dad.

"None of us are hideous. Life would be much easier if we were." Dad dug into his stroganoff. "She likes the showmanship. Danu has always been the most dramatic of us."

He paused and focused on his food for a moment before setting down his fork. "Evie."

The way his voice sounded gave me pause. "Should we have one final meal together in peace? Then we can discuss how this most recent thing will fuck up our lives?"

Dad and Rowan exchanged a glance. Finally, Dad gave me a sharp nod. "That's a fine idea. Should we invite your mother?"

"The more the merrier." Speaking of inviting people… "Where are Simone and Garrett?"

Rowan carefully focused on cutting his beef. "They'll be back shortly."

I watched him. "Rowan."

"They are fine, Evie. I promise. They're temporarily out, acting in your best interests."

"According to whom?" Now I was definitely suspicious.

"Everyone," the Lord said simply.

"So now everyone is making decisions for me?" Anger made my hands shake. "How is this different from what I left?"

Rowan's jaw tightened. "Unlike Caelan," he said, fury vibrating in his voice, "I am not trying to force you into doing anything that might make you uncomfortable. I am, however, getting something back. Something I know you've missed while you've been with me."

What could he possibly think I missed more than my land? "I have plenty of clothing," I mumbled. "There's nothing in my house I need right now."

A vibrant streak of purple and orange shot through the colorful skies. My fork clattered to the plate. The bright *kraa kraa* sound of a raven sent tears flooding my eyes. I stood so quickly, my chair thumped back and fell, then took off running toward the two birds flying straight toward me.

"Poe! Fee!" My voice broke as Fee zoomed in my direction, sparks of fire flashing from her tail. She screeched to a halt, wings spread twice the length of my body. Poe circled around us a few times before landing on my shoulder, careful to keep his claws from puncturing my skin.

He croaked and nuzzled my cheek with his feathery head. "Evie. Evie. Miss Evie."

I stroked his silky back. "I missed you too."

Fee was so large she could no longer sit on my shoulder. "And you, beautiful thing," I crooned. "Look how big you've gotten."

Fee made an adorable trilling sound. I held my arm out. She gently alighted, her weight less than I expected. I brought her closer and rubbed my cheek against her head. I meant to get them out before I left, but everything happened so quickly, and when I woke up and realized they were still with Caelan, I asked Moira to go over and get them.

Caelan had flat out refused. Poe could have escaped at any time, but he would never abandon Fee. If something had happened, Poe would have come to me, and to ensure they were still being treated well, Dad had poked his head in a few times.

Caelan might be a lot of things, but he would never harm someone or something who was no threat to him. A male and female came into view, one tall and lean, the other slim and blonde. The lean man had his arms around the woman's waist, and they both limped toward me.

"Simone?" Fee flitted from my arm and zoomed toward Simone and Garrett.

"Injured." Poe croaked. "Hurt."

I swore under my breath and glanced toward Rowan who was already jogging my way. Dad followed behind.

I hurried toward them, noticing Simone had something tucked into the crook of her elbow. When I got closer, that something leapt from her arms, rattling its traps as it launched itself toward me.

An odd noise warbled from its throat. I gasped and reached out, wincing as the ceramic pot slammed against my hands. "Seymour?"

"And Hannah," Garrett said, holding up a smaller plant.

Seymour reached for Hannah, so I took her from Garrett's blood grip, grimacing at the smear of red on the side of her pot.

I had a million questions, but Garrett and Simone looked like they'd walked out of a war zone. Dad reached them before Rowan, his swirling eyes taking in the situation.

"I see," he said, magic glowing in his palms. "If you allow it, I can heal you."

"Please," Simone gasped.

Garrett let go of her waist but kept his hand at her elbow as she limped over to my father. Her face was covered with soot and scratches. The blouse she wore had a long tear in one sleeve and several still smoking holes. Simone's jeans were in shreds, and she was missing a shoe.

Garrett was in worse form. His shirt was completely gone, his honed chest covered in burns and bruises. He had a split lip and a black eye, and a long cut across one cheek. His knuckles were bruised and bloody, and I was pretty sure that was bone poking out from a hole in his pants. It was a miracle he was able to walk.

"How—" I shook my head. "It doesn't matter. I'll save my questions for later. For now, I'm glad you're in one piece."

Dad reached out both hands and touched Simone and Garrett at the same time. Both sagged with relief a moment later.

"Thank you," Garrett said.

Simone flung out her arms and brought my dad in for a tight hug. "Evie's dad, you're a real one."

He chuckled awkwardly and patted her on the back before stepping away. "It seems you two have a story to tell."

Simone held up a finger. "Wait. There's more."

Rowan grimaced. "Is it the police?"

Garrett snorted. "You know me well enough to know I leave no witnesses, Lord."

I blinked at Garrett. "Don't forget you're under new management."

A dark-haired female came into view. All thoughts fled from my head as her lips widened into a grin.

I shoved Seymour and Hannah into Rowan's arms, burst into tears, and took off running. Moira and I collided, both of us talking and crying at the same time.

"You look—"

"How did you—"

"When did—"

We stopped talking and held each other. Moira smelled of herbs and magic, and it was the best thing I'd smelled in over a month. She was as thin as she always was, but her frame held a coiled power I usually never noticed. Moira was going through things just like I was, though she held those closer to her than I did these days, even with my gentle but insistent prodding.

"I missed you so much." With a gentle squeeze, I stepped back and examined my vampire friend. Her eyes held a haunted look she normally kept hidden. "Moira?"

She smiled. "There's plenty of time to talk later." Moira looped an arm through mine and tugged me toward Rowan. "Let's go have our reunion."

Sixteen

After a massive lunch and three more pitchers of strawberry lemonade, Rowan leaned forward. "Tell me, Garrett. After your adventures, are we at war with Caelan?"

Garrett's grin was a cold, smug thing. "Strength recognizes strength. There were no life-altering injuries, and we only took things Evie has a claim to."

Rowan chuckled. "And he forgot to alter his wards to keep you out."

Garrett inclined his head. "And there's that. Technically, we did nothing wrong. We came onto Keep lands because we were not barred and had not yet signed our separation paperwork."

Dad laughed.

"I'll expect a courier today," Rowan said dryly.

"We took Hannah, and Seymour, and Poe and Fee followed," Garrett added. "That is one freaky smart bird you have, Evie."

"How'd you travel with them?"

Moira wiggled her fingers in a wave. "Potions, but I am now officially out of ingredients. There's a small stash left, but expect at least six months before I can make any more."

"And the birds?" I asked. Garrett and Simone were easily

explained by the travel potions, but Poe and Fee had arrived right after.

Moira grinned. "I traveled with Fee. Poe got here on his own."

I eyed the raven playing with Fee high above the Keep. "Did he now?"

"That he did. Poe is holding a wealth of secrets inside that glowing little body."

Poe dove underneath Fee and rose up a second later, coming so close to Fee she screeched with delight.

Moira smiled. "Those two are inseparable."

Simone leaned back in her chair. "You should expect a visit from the other Lord soon."

Garrett winced. "Furious is an understatement. The bastard used guns on us."

Rowan blinked. "Guns?"

Simone's nod was grim. "No silver bullets, but they still hurt like a bitch. We had to get the bullets out before we used the potions. Otherwise, we couldn't concentrate enough to travel."

"The Caelan you know is gone, Evie." Garrett's eyes held sympathy. "I'm sorry."

Maybe I never knew him at all. "I've only known him for a year or so. You've known him most of your lives. Would you say he's different, or did he change himself for me?"

Simone and Garrett exchanged a look.

"Ah," I nodded. "I knew the Caelan he wanted me to see."

Simone leaned forward. "No. Don't do that. We all put on a face when we're in the wooing stage."

Garrett snorted. "No one says woo." He kept glancing at Rowan, a slight wrinkle in his forehead.

Simone tossed a grape at him. "It's the perfect word. Caelan was wooing her in his unhinged, slightly psychotic way."

"I'm with Simone," Dad said. "Wooing implies trying to win the favor or love of another person. Caelan went full speed ahead with marriage plans before Evie liked him."

Simone laughed. "Those were fun times."

I tossed a grape at her this time. "Look at us now."

Garrett was still staring at Rowan. I glanced at the Lord and watched him shift uncomfortably. "Everything okay?" I asked.

Both men turned their eyes to me. "Fine," they snapped in unison.

My hand stilled in mid-air, the fork halfway to my mouth. "Yes," I said slowly. "Everything seems awesome."

Simone took another helping of cheese and grapes. "Regardless of whatever this is, Caelan is pissed. He's angry at you; he's angry at us." She slowly shook her head. "But he wants to tear Rowan's head from his shoulders."

Rowan chuckled. "He's welcome to try."

Garrett leaned forward, still wearing that intense look. "You have much to lose, Lord. Caelan has never willingly relinquished his possessions."

A ring of gold glowed in Rowan's eyes. "Evie is not a possession. Neither is Fee or Poe or Evie's carnivorous plants."

Seymour, who'd been surprisingly docile, waved his traps around and thumped over to Rowan, hopping in his pot a few times until the Lord picked him up and stroked one of his traps.

Seymour let out an odd purring noise and bumped Rowan's chest.

But guilt flooded me. Caelan and Seymour were friends, weren't they?

Simone leaned over. "He came willingly. Hannah as well."

"What happened, Simone?" The words were a whisper.

Simone jerked her head at Moira. Both women rose, Moira's cool fingers touching my shoulder. "Come on," she said softly.

Both women linked arms with me and guided me away from the table.

Empathy filled Simone's eyes. "Shifters are complicated creatures. Lords even more so. I know you love him, Evie, but wolves are highly intelligent and crafty creatures. They approach challenges with intricate plans and will do whatever it takes to win."

My heart lurched at her words. "You think I was just a challenge to him."

Moira shot Simone a recriminating look.

"No," Simone breathed. And just as my shoulders relaxed, she sighed. "And yes. He cared about you, loved you even, but of course you were a challenge. You embarrassed him in front of all his peers, and it infuriated him, but it was also a red flag waved in front of an angry bull. That was the start of everything. He was obsessed with you, and obsession is never a healthy way to begin a relationship."

"I saw him first," I admitted. "When I was at lunch. Later that night, I found him dying in the woods."

Simone nodded. "It took him some time to connect the dots. Adding you to his Keep would have been a boon for him, both as the Pack Alpha and as a Lord. And a boon to the other shifters."

Moira's upper lip curled into a snarl even as I wanted to curl in on myself. "I've been a fool," I whispered.

Moira tugged me to a stop underneath a large willow tree still in its spring greenery. We sat underneath, Moira leaning her head on my shoulder. "What does it matter how it started?" she asked. "Shouldn't we only be concerned with the end?"

"Everything should matter," Simone said, tucking her feet underneath her thighs. "Beginning, middle, and end."

"Simone is right," I said. "But it's not all Caelan's fault."

Fury vibrated Moira's thin frame. "He said you were flawed. Who speaks to someone they love like that?"

"He was also under Lugh's influence."

"That's no excuse. We all know how magic like that works. Just because you don't say the words out loud doesn't mean you don't believe them. Caelan spoke what his heart felt."

And that was the truth I kept trying to avoid, but I knew the inevitable day would come when I finally took that truth into my heart and made the decision that would change everything permanently. I was here with Rowan, but my house was still in

Joy Springs. It still belonged to me. The shop still stood, thanks to my friends' goodwill, but that would change soon, too.

I could go back any time I wanted.

But seeing Caelan again felt like a bruise I kept poking. The look in his eyes, the words he said to me, I wasn't sure I'd ever forgive him.

Nor was I sure I should, but there was more to this now. There was the male sitting at the table with my father who'd taken me with him when he didn't have to and gave me a space to rest and heal. He'd given me far more than I'd ever given him, trusted me with more than Caelan ever had. Rowan still had secrets, many of them, but he owed me nothing when I hadn't given him all that much of myself either.

"All wolves are like Caelan?" I asked Simone.

"Every wolf is different, but they're all crafty and have a one-track mind when they see something they want. Different hierarchies exist as well. A Lord is much different than an Omega, like me."

"What about other animals?"

Simone went still. A smile played on her lips. "Like...a bear, for instance?"

Moira jerked upright and turned her dark eyes to me. "Is Rowan a bear?" she hissed.

"You can't tell anyone," I whispered.

"Oh my gods. That's why he is so damn friendly all the time!"

Simone snorted. "Bears are often mistaken as solitary creatures when nothing could be further from the truth. They're highly social, but they like to choose who they're social with. But," she continued, her eyes sparkling with amusement, "they are clever when it comes to choosing their mates and once they've chosen, they do not falter from the course until they have no other choice. Bears are also highly territorial and follow their chosen mate to protect them from others."

"Is that why Rowan always seemed to be there when Evie needed him?" Moira asked, sliding a curious look Rowan's way.

Simone shrugged. "Rowan has always been a curious creature. He's driven as much by the man as he is by the bear, but he's secretive as well. There is more to him than meets the eye. Just like all the other Lords, but I've always suspected Rowan hides how powerful he is under the guise of charm and peaceful intentions."

"Why didn't you ever go for him?" Moira asked.

Jealousy roared within me, surprising me with its intensity. Simone's eyes widened when she sensed it, even as a slow grin pulled her lips up. "Rowan is attractive, sure, but he's not my type. I'm also an Omega. Leaving my Pack is extraordinarily difficult."

"But you did it for Evie," Moira pointed out.

Simone inclined her head. "True, but I lost faith in Caelan. My power draws me to those who most need it. An Omega is born to serve, but Caelan refused my power more often than not."

"What exactly is your power?" I asked. Simone had always wielded most of her power with a clipboard and a tablet. I'd never seen her expend any true magic since I'd known her.

She held out her hands. "It's easier to show you if you'll allow me."

Moira and I shrugged and placed our hands in hers.

Nothing happened for a few seconds. Simone closed her eyes and told us to do the same.

"Think of something that hurt you. An emotional wound is best."

"Will you be able to see what the wound is?" Moira asked.

Simone and I both cracked an eye open at the question. "No," Simone said, a frown on her mouth. "I'll only be able to sense your distress."

"Alright then." Moira exhaled.

We closed our eyes once more, and I thought about Caelan. Many emotional wounds marked my life, but his betrayal was the freshest. Every time my memory went back to that day in the square, pain squeezed my heart in an iron grip. I awoke most nights in a damp sweat, tears in my eyes. The last thing anyone wanted to think about themselves was how flawed they were, but Caelan had managed to take the things about myself I hated the most and bring them to the forefront, to twist the knife in so deep I couldn't free myself.

That pain roared to the front of my mind, bringing fresh tears and hurt to the surface, but a moment later a gentle rain of sky-blue magic washed over me, and suddenly, the pain wasn't as fresh. Things didn't hurt as much. I could see past those wounds to the fragile person underneath, the woman who only wanted to be loved.

Sometimes when we were trapped by pain and hurt, we couldn't see the reason why. All we felt was the pain. But with Simone's magic washing that agony away, I could see myself again, first as a child flinching from my mother's sharp words, then the sting of being abandoned, and later as a married woman trying to wash away the images of my husband with another woman. Scotland came and went, and even that night in the heather field wasn't as painful as normal, flashing forward to meeting Caelan and my loneliness, and how he'd washed that away and brought with him a mix of fear and trepidation and love all mixed up in a tangled knot.

I wanted to be loved so badly, I'd forgotten that love didn't always mean pain. I'd somehow managed to convince myself that loving someone meant constantly questioning yourself, your motives, and someone else's motives. My magic and background also factored in, and when my origins were revealed, I wondered whether Caelan had always wanted me for me or if he'd always suspected something was off about me.

But now I could look at that without the sharp pain accompanying the thoughts.

And my answer was yes, he'd known. Had it mattered to him was another question I couldn't answer yet. Like most of the Lords, he craved power, and I could give him more than he'd ever known, but when I was able to see things a little more clearly, away from that haze of my broken heart, I knew the things I could give him weren't the only reasons he was with me.

Caelan had loved me, maybe still did, in his own way. Doubts were normal, but some doubts could not be overcome, no matter the pretty words you used to cover them up. He worried about his future line, and whether the children we made together would be something monstrous or something that might conquer the heavens.

No matter how powerful Caelan was or might become, the thought of a child more powerful than him or one who might not look or act the way he expected terrified him.

As Simone's magic washed through me, tears fell from my eyes, long suppressed anger and grief giving way to realization and healing. Things with him were unresolved, but they wouldn't stay that way forever. When her magic trickled to a halt, I knew what I had to do.

Moira's face was wet with tears, her slender body trembling. I scooted closer and wrapped an arm around her waist. When her eyes opened, she focused on Simone.

"Caelan is an idiot for letting you go. Your power is—" Her throat worked. "You're a healer, Simone. I hope you know that."

Simone's lower lip wobbled. "Any time you want to see me, Moira, just give me a call or come by." She let out a heavy sigh. "It might be a while before we figure out where we're going next, but you'll know the moment I do."

Everything hinged on the decisions I made. Simone gave our hands a gentle squeeze and let go, closing her eyes and leaning against the trunk. A happy smile curved her lips. "Thank you. It's been far too long since I've used my gifts."

"Have you thought about asking Rowan? I've only met a couple of his people, but I know Rowan well enough to know he'll utilize talented people."

Simone cracked an eye open. "I'm loyal to you."

I didn't understand. "Thank you for that, but one doesn't have anything to do with the other, does it?"

"It does," Moira said. "If Simone was still in a Pack, but she's not."

Simone opened her other eye and frowned. But then she slowly sat up, her lips parting.

"Free agent, baby," Moira said. "You can start charging for your services."

Simone looked at me. "Don't ask me. It's your gift."

"Yes, but you're my…" Her brow knit together. "I'm sworn to you."

"Only in that you have to protect my people. There's nothing in our contract about acting as a freelancer." I nudged her with an elbow. "I'm not Caelan. Use your magic wherever you have permission to do so. Charge for it. Hell, start a business. I might be the 'official' fae queen, but as you can see, things are a little shaky right now." I still hadn't told them what was happening with my rule or what I'd promised my mother and father.

Time enough to deal with that later.

Rowan caught my eye and waved us back over, but when Moira wandered toward them, Simone tugged on my hand. "Evie. Stay back for a moment. There's something I need to tell you."

Concerned, I stopped and turned. Simone's expression was serious, her eyes soft. "Everything okay?"

"Yes," she assured me, "but there's something you should know. I meant to tell you earlier, but other things were happening, and…" she exhaled. "Well, this will be hard to hear and might change things, but you deserve to know."

My heartbeat intensified, and my palms went clammy. "Is this about Caelan?"

She tugged me down, and I sat once more, my back against the tree trunk.

"I'm sorry, Evie." When she opened her mouth again, the words she said didn't register at first. But when they did, the world fell out from under my feet.

• • •

Dad was looking over our shoulders as we retook our seats. A tingle of familiar magic shimmered from behind, revealing my mother, casually dressed in a pair of trousers and a silk blouse, the same color as her eyes. Her hair was loose and curled, and her makeup, which she never needed, carefully applied.

Mom only dressed like that when she dealt with humans. She smiled at me as she came over, taking the seat Dad offered her. Poe and Fee had disappeared somewhere, and I made a mental note to speak to the raven to see if Fee was comfortable revealing herself to Cliona. I remembered the day I took the phoenix home and how worried I was the entire time as I waited for her to hatch. Mom had eventually revealed herself to not be the monster we all believed her to be, but Fee had never met her. I wondered if they would like each other.

"Evie?" Mom's brow knitted with concern. "Everything alright?"

"Lots on my mind," I said, smiling to wipe the worry from her expression. "Dad has something to tell us, and it's been itching at him for hours now."

"Danu," Mom said. "We all felt her rise."

"Something poisons the earth," Dad began. "But the magic is more subtle than we would be."

Mom's lips pursed. "You think it's a spell then. From witches?"

Dad nodded. "Much harder to pin down the identity of a witch than it is a god or goddess."

"Every witch has a power signature," Moira said. "If you show me what you're talking about, I might be able to help."

"Are there more places with visible damage?" I asked Dad. "Everything I saw was under the surface."

"I haven't seen them all." He turned to Moira. "If you're willing, I can quickly transport you to those places to see if you can get a read from them. Time is of the essence. The outskirts of Rowan's land are damaged. Every day we delay, the Lord's power will weaken."

My attention snapped to Rowan. "Are you okay?"

"I've felt nothing so far," the Lord said.

"The magic is new and spread all over the country," Dad said, "concentrated at the edges of two of the Lord's territories. In a few days the Lords in the affected areas will know something is wrong."

"Caelan?" I asked.

"No. Your healer Lord."

"Ben?" I closed my eyes. "Shit. He might realize it sooner. Ben is sensitive to magic. We should call him when we're finished with this meeting."

"They targeted who they perceive to be the less dangerous Lords," Mom mused.

Rowan bristled, making Mom laugh. "Those of us here know you are a deadly thing, but the face you show to the public is that of a friendly, peaceable Lord. Ben is untried and known as a Healer. Fae healers are not warriors." Her eyes glittered. "Our kind continually underestimates how powerful the Lords are. Perhaps it is a good thing you and Ben were targeted first. This gives us more time to plan and discover who's responsible."

"Any ideas?" Moira said, reaching for a cracker.

Dad shook his head. "Lugh is trapped. Titania is dead. There are others who do not support your claim to the throne, but they've remained relatively quiet."

"So it could be anyone." Unsurprising. Nothing was easy these days.

Dad inclined his head. "Mom will give you a list."

"How mundane," Moira drawled. "A list of potential criminals."

Rowan had stayed uncharacteristically silent. "What's the purpose of the spell?"

Dad's jaw tightened. "That is why I'm here. The spell will weaken your claim on the land, eventually shattering the bond."

Rowan paled. I reached under the table and took his hand. "And mine?"

Dad shook his head. "Your blood will always be the wildcard. The magic is anathema to Danu. Getting too close weakens her."

"She's a goddess," Simone said thoughtfully. "If this is a spell created by witches, how could it overpower someone like her?"

"Whoever is targeting her knows her weaknesses and designed the spell to keep her from destroying it before the work is done." Mom poured herself a glass of lemonade.

"Targeting Danu targets me because of my Floromancy, but the spells were placed right on the edges of the Lords' borders, increasing the odds they wouldn't notice until it was too late to do anything. Whoever this is targets the Lords, too."

Dad nodded. "Likely. The fae are making a play for the land and cannot take it when bonded to another, this includes Danu. Assume, Evie, they're trying to wrest yours away too."

"I've felt nothing," I admitted, "but I haven't been the best at bonding with Donovan's old lands."

Dad rose, holding his hand out for Mom to take. "Then I suggest you start soon." His ancient gaze rested on Rowan. "I would speak with you once more before we leave."

Simone and Moira both frowned at my father. "You know what happened the first time you started keeping secrets from Evie," the vampire said.

Dad laughed. "Relax, little vampire who is more than she seems, all my secrets will soon be revealed. Think of this as more fatherly advice than secrets. I will return at sunrise to escort you to those foul places that need your sharp eyes."

Moira nodded, watching him warily.

Rowan's jaw tightened, but he rose and followed my father. Mom glided over and brushed a kiss against my cheek. "I've seen Caelan," she murmured. "He travels this way." When she rose, her eyes were laughing. "But your vampire refused to give him any more potions, so his travel is mundane."

Moira's innocent expression didn't fool me.

"He will be here soon." Mom cupped my chin. "I want the best for you, Evie, but I will not stand in your way on a choice like this."

My throat tightened.

"A bit of advice if you don't mind?"

I nodded and waited. Mom rarely offered guidance, our past still very much a tender thing we tiptoed around.

"You can love someone so much your heart aches, but it does not mean they are right for you. Someone can pluck your strings like a master harpist but every once in a while, play a discordant note that echoes. Listen to those notes, Evie. Listen for that echo." She dropped to her knees and took my face in her hands. "The world has been a harsh place for you, darling. Think about what you want and who you want standing beside you when peace finally comes. Think about the people you've never questioned, the places that make your heart sing. Even if you're standing alone at the end, it doesn't mean you'll be lonely."

Tears burned the back of my eyes. "You don't think I should go back to him."

Mom's eyes burned with love. "I think he became your world when your world was small. But you've seen universes since then, my darling—experienced different kinds of love. I want you to have someone who stands by your side no matter what challenges are thrown before you, someone who lets you make mistakes without judgment, someone who looks at you like you are the sunrise and sunset. Choose someone who does not choose their crown over you. Choose someone who would never make you feel small. If that is Caelan, then you know what you need to do. But if you hold doubt in your heart, do not take that final step. When you know for sure, there will be no doubt. A choice will present itself soon, Evie—one that will change the trajectory of your life. The decision will not come from your head. It has to come from your heart."

With that, Mom disappeared in a shower of light, leaving me more confused than ever.

"Is she always that confusing?" Moira murmured.

Simone let out a snort, followed by a giggle. My lips twitched, but I couldn't hold the laughter in either. Moira belly laughed.

"Can you believe I'm the queen of these people?" I cackled. "Especially when I've always been so bad at solving riddles?"

Simone wheezed.

Moira cackled. "Remember that puzzle that sat on your coffee table for eighteen months?"

I had tears coming out of my eyes. "Puzzles are dumb!"

"That's because you put the corners together first, then work your way inside! Don't approach it like it's a Salvador Dalí!"

"Those are different from riddles," I say through bouts of laughter. "I would have put it together eventually if I hadn't lost some of the pieces."

Moira rolled her eyes. "It's still in the office if you want to try again."

"No!" I barked, sending Simone and Moira into another fit of laughter.

Dark things awaited us on the horizon, but for now we had each other, a gorgeous sunset, and a full pitcher of strawberry lemonade.

All the crises could wait for a little while longer.

CHAPTER

Seventeen

ROWAN

ernunnos walked far enough away to prevent the others from overhearing.

"How much do I need to worry?" I asked. Jealousy and bitterness came at people like me all the time. For all our people claimed to want a leader, being led tended to rankle a large portion of the population. Even though I was considered one of the gentler Lords, I still fended off what I felt to be an egregious number of assassination and coup attempts.

What I would give for a life away from politics and leading those who did not wish to be led.

Evie's father watched me, a faint smile on his face as though he knew which direction my thoughts had gone. "Your tie to your land is stronger than the other Lords."

Unsurprising he wouldn't give me a direct answer. "Do you have any practical advice, or did you bring me away from everyone else to give me more riddles?" I studied my fingernails. "I do so hate riddles."

He pinned me with that ancient, unforgiving stare. "You wish me to be direct?"

I threw out my hands. "Yes! Just say what you're thinking or tell me how to fix this." Not that he would. Dealing with the fae felt like standing in an avalanche of sand, trying to count the grains before they fell past.

His guise changed from that of a young man into the terrifying visage of the leader of the Wild Hunt. Enormous antlers grew from his head, tipped with bioluminescent moss and tiny mushrooms. His clothing morphed from athletic wear into soft leather breeches and a vest strung with bones. A god stood before me, any pretense of friendliness gone with his t-shirt and bare feet. I might think I knew him, but Cernunnos was crafty and fickle, manipulative and willing to do whatever he had to in order to protect those he loves.

"You and Evangeline are stronger together. If you hope to wrest your lands from this dark influence, you should cement your bond, allow her a claim on your land, and merge her untended property to yours. You would secure the largest stretch of territory in this country, wipe the influence from your lands, and become untouchable to the other Lords as well as less powerful fae."

I stared at Cernunnos for a long moment, stunned. "You wish me to become king." I'd have no issue with allowing Evie's mark on my lands, but it would be her choice and, so far, she'd chosen not to because she cared about how I felt and what I needed. She had not yet realized that her mark was already on my land, her touch stamped deep on its Lord.

"There are worse choices," Cernunnos said.

"Not exactly a rousing endorsement," I spluttered. "Your daughter is still thinking of returning to Caelan. I will not force her into a bond when she loves another man."

"We both know a bond like that can be forced."

"But it can be formed without another's knowledge." I shook my head vehemently. "I will lose her if I do such a thing. Tell me, Cernunnos, is that why you wish me to pursue such a path, so she will hate me and be free to choose among the undoubtedly numerous better choices you have awaiting her back in your lands?"

"My lands are her lands, too, Lord. There are no other men, as you say. Her heart is no contest. She won't give it out as a prize for pleasing her. Evie will choose as she sees fit."

"And if she chooses Caelan?"

The god's eyes sparkled. "I would hope the man who loves her will convince her why that is a bad choice."

I swore. "If you are through tormenting me, you may leave."

The god's mocking laughter lingered long after he disappeared.

I let out a slow breath and tilted my head up to the darkening sky. Secrets had gotten us into this mess. Would the truth set us free?

Eighteen

Moira, Simone, and Garrett had accepted Rowan's hospitality and were staying on the other side of the Keep, a few miles away from Rowan's main residence. We planned to reconvene tomorrow to figure out what we could do to stop this disaster in its tracks. Rowan would call Ben in the morning, but tonight it was only us, dining outside under the stars.

Where it was normally easy between us, tonight held a fine thread of tension, the many things we left unsaid lying between us. I was on my third glass of wine and should have been wiser. This was the stuff Mom and Hazel had invented, and it had a kick. Such a kick, my tongue threatened to wag, and that rarely went well for me.

But Rowan had imbibed too, his third glass sitting almost empty by his plate. We dined on beef stew tonight, served with a delicious crusty bread. I asked to meet his chef, but Rowan demurred.

"He's shy," was all he said, but there was a twinkle in his eyes.

"Are you keeping me from your people for a reason?" I asked, wincing as the words tumbled from my lips.

Rowan blinked in surprise. "Evie. No. I—you came here

wounded and alone. I thought seeing everyone all at once might overwhelm you."

"I've been here a month!"

Rowan laughed at my outraged tone. "Yes, and in that month you've been barely alive. You've done more these past few days than you've done in weeks."

My nostrils flared. The urge to argue with him almost overwhelmed me, but he was right.

Rowan grinned. "There's that spark. I wondered when it would come back."

"You provoke me on purpose," I grumbled.

He held his hands up and leaned back. "I answered a question! But your memories are wrong. You've already met some of my people."

I narrowed my eyes, racking my brain for the answer. "The artist."

"And everyone in the town square. I have far more paranormals than just shifters. My territory has long been considered a haven for others who are different."

"More different than a Chimera?" I said with a rueful chuckle.

"You'd be surprised," he said cryptically, "but no, there are no Chimeras here. You and your Barrett are the only ones I know of, though I'm sure if anyone knows more, you'd be the one to ask."

Moira's words came back to me. "Caelan is on his way."

"I'm surprised he isn't already here."

"Moira wouldn't give him a potion."

We grinned at each other before Rowan's smile faded. "He will hold a grudge, Evie. For all of this."

I looked down at my clasped fingers. "I know. He hasn't declared war yet, so that's a plus."

Rowan snorted. "He won't declare war while you live on my lands. He comes here to take you home." He eyed me. "If you still consider Joy Springs your home."

Rowan poured us both a glass of wine, laughing when I sighed and took it. "I have some special drops in the kitchen. Remind me and I'll give you some before you go to bed. They'll stop a hangover in its tracks."

I perked up. "Did Mom give them to you?"

He winked. "I'll never reveal my sources."

I studied him, the booze loosening my tongue. "You have a way with people, Rowan. You lead with hope, not fear. Your people look at you with kinship. It's admirable."

Rowan swallowed, his hazel eyes sparking a vivid green in the low candlelight. "I don't know how to lead any other way. Instilling fear in someone is not the way to win their loyalty."

"Caelan's people do not fear him. Not exactly. He has never responded with violence to anyone I've ever seen."

Rowan's eyes flashed and his knuckles tightened around his glass. "Caelan is many things," he said, which was no response at all.

I leaned forward. "What are you not saying?"

My fingers itched to reach out and trace the firm line of his jaw, brush his hair away from his face. I clenched my hand into a fist, but Rowan...he noticed.

He leaned closer and took my hand, gently opening my fist. He traced a symbol on my palm and pressed my hand to his stubbled cheek. "Touch me whenever you like, Evie."

His eyes closed as my thumb rubbed over his cheek, tracing down to his full lips.

"What is happening between us?" I whispered.

Rowan leaned closer, brushing his lips over mine. His touch sent fire skittering down my nerves. He reached down and jerked my chair toward him, gripping me by the waist and hauling me into his lap. One hand slid through my hair, tugging my head back to grant him easier access to my lips. The kiss deepened, his tongue sliding in my mouth.

A low moan escaped me, Rowan's grip tightening in my hair.

I pressed my palms against his muscled chest, fingers gripping his sweater. "There's something between us," I said against his lips. "Something different."

He stood, gripping me around the hips. I laced my arms around his neck and wrapped my legs around his waist. Rowan kissed me senseless once more, his lips trailing down my throat, leaving a searing trail of heat down my skin.

"You're right," he said, holding me tight against him. His head rested against my collarbone. "I'd like to show you something."

I ran my fingers through his hair, tracing the lines of his beautiful face. "I didn't realize this when I first met you, but you are beautiful, Rowan. Inside and out."

I felt him smile against my skin. "Prettier than the little wolf Lord?"

I laughed, glad we could joke about him, at least a little. "Less scary for sure."

He still held me, his grip warm and firm. "You were surrounded by enemies on all sides. A friendly face was warranted."

I laid my cheek against his hair. "If I haven't said it yet, thank you for everything you've done."

His arms tightened. "You never need to thank me."

I let Rowan carry me through his lands, enjoying the feeling of safety and security. He stopped several minutes later, gently setting me down next to a large oak tree and a small pond.

He tugged me to the ground, and we sat facing each other.

I looked around, realizing I'd never been here before. I'd walked a lot of his land, but 1,500 acres was too far for one person to explore in a short period of time. Moonlight shimmered on the water, the only sound a soft breeze rustling the branches.

I broke the silence. "You're making me nervous."

Rowan smiled, but it was a hesitant one, his eyes wary. "I'm about to show you something no one else knows."

I watched him, wondering if I'd regret coming here, curious if he was going to break my heart with this newest secret. Whatever was happening with us, I felt exhilarated, but terrified, scared, and overwhelmed. I wasn't ready. There was no closure with

Caelan, and I owed it to both of us to see the ruins of our relationship through to what might be the bitter end.

When Rowan saw my expression, he huffed a laugh and reached for my hands. "No. Evie. This affects me far more than you. I only wanted to be honest with you. I'd like there to be no more secrets. Not between us. There is something more than friendship here, but you are my friend first. No matter what happens, I hope you will always be my friend."

My heart melted. "Of course I will be your friend. Always."

"I would never do anything to hurt you. Never."

I nodded. Despite his words, I still felt apprehensive. "I feel the same."

Rowan nodded and scooted back, slowly rising to his feet. "My mother was not a shifter."

"Alright," I said slowly. "It doesn't matter to me who your parents were."

A faint smile before a shiver of magic flowed over my skin followed by a flash of light. Where Roman had once stood, a large white owl hovered.

I sucked in a breath. *"Rowan."*

He sailed over. Without thinking, I held my arm out, just like I did with Poe. Rowan landed on my forearm, wicked claws curling carefully over my skin. I reached up and stroked the downy feathers atop his head. "Aren't you a pretty thing," I cooed.

Rowan rubbed his cheek against mine and flew away. Another shiver of magic and a flash of light, and a woman stood before me, Moira, this time.

My heart dropped into my stomach. I stared at him, the words falling right out of my head.

Rowan shifted again, this time into the guise of an eagle. A sharp cry came from his throat as he circled overhead.

Was he…?

No, he couldn't be. Rowan circled a few more times and came in for a landing, shifting into his human form.

Still fully clothed, thank goodness. My eyes narrowed as I shifted through the potential. "You're part fae."

He sat down, facing me once more. "My mother's name is Bea. She's a shapeshifter. My father is a bear shifter."

I stared at him open mouthed. "Can you become anything?"

"I haven't tried everything, but so far there've been no barriers."

The possibilities were endless. Rowan, much like me, could be the perfect spy. No wonder he kept this secret from everyone. "None of the other Lords know?"

He shook his head. "They do not allow mixed blood Lords, though I know for a fact Ben is one, so that rule seems to get tossed when it doesn't work for them."

"Why would you trust me with something like that?" I rubbed a hand over my face. "I know what it's like to keep such a secret. You've given me your life, Rowan. Why?"

"Because there's something else you should know."

That spot in my chest warmed once more. I touched my heart, our eyes meeting. And when Rowan opened his mouth to speak, I suspected I knew the truth he was about to utter.

The wards around Rowan's property boomed.

The Lord bowed his head and expelled a heavy sigh.

"He's here, isn't he?" I asked softly.

Rowan didn't answer, merely stood, and offered me his hand.

And together, we turned to confront the inevitable.

CHAPTER

Nineteen

ROWAN

I should have told her. The words repeated in my head over and over. Dread pooled in my veins as we walked, the insistent pounding of the wards indicative of Caelan's rising temper.

He couldn't break them; they were reinforced by Evie's father, but he could make my life difficult if he continued trying to get in. Evie walked beside me, her fingers linked with mine. She made no move to tug her hand away—a hopeful sign, even though I felt the slight tremor in her body and could hear the pounding of her heart. She was frightened and nervous, but there was a thread of confusion running through her emotions.

The confusion might save us.

It took several minutes to reach the front. Evie let go of my hand and walked ahead, her eyes on Caelan. The other Lord straightened when he spotted her, his hands sliding into his pockets to affect a casual posture.

Caelan felt anything but casual. Wolves and bears were nothing alike, but a predator recognized another predator. His eyes glowed bright gold as he looked at her, but his face was a careful mask. Fool. If he hoped to get her back, he should be wearing his heart on his sleeve.

Evie wasn't a woman made for blank expressions and cold hearts.

I stopped a good distance away, far enough to give her privacy, but close enough to intercede if anything went wrong. Also close enough to overhear their conversation.

I was a good man, but I was no saint.

Evie stopped a couple of feet away from Caelan, watching him carefully. Her long dark hair blew in the wind, sweeping away from her neck in a tangle of waves. She'd changed for dinner, jeans and a green cashmere quarter zip, ankle boots with thick wool socks, and a wool undershirt. This far away, Evie looked like a beautiful human woman.

"Come out and meet me," Caelan rumbled, eyes still glowing.

"We'll speak here," Evie said with a steady voice.

"Afraid of me now?"

"No. I haven't been afraid of you for a while now."

Pride rose in me.

Caelan didn't like those words. His eyes narrowed. "I've come here to bring you home."

"I'm capable of bringing myself home when I'm ready to go."

"You don't want to come back with me?"

Evie snorted. "We are no longer together. You broke up with me over a month ago, or have you forgotten?"

Caelan's nostrils flared. "I was under the influence of a god, Evie. How can you not see that?"

"I saw perfectly fine," Evie snapped. "Do you take me for an idiot? Lugh's magic was not foolproof. We both know how it works. Those doubts existed in you long before Lugh came to town."

He threw his hands out. "Yes, I had doubts. Everyone has doubts. You and I are about to be married."

"Were."

Caelan blew out a breath. "Children have to be part of the equation. I am a Lord. You are a Queen. There has to be a succession plan."

Wrong thing to say. Evie's posture stiffened. "A succession plan?" she said softly.

Caelan took a step closer. "Don't turn your nose up. We have to think about the future. What will happen if we don't have an heir fit to take our crowns?"

I bit down the smile threatening to bloom.

"You don't have a crown," Evie snarled.

Caelan waved his hand. "But I will. And you do. Even if we walked away from each other, you would still need to have a succession plan for whoever comes next."

"Unlike you, I don't think the same. If I had a child, I'd want him or her to be healthy first. Then I'd want them to be loved. I'd want them to grow up in a happy home, and I'd want them to wake up every single day and know that their father and I will be there when they walk out of their room. I'd take my crown off and melt it in a fire if it ever came between me and my child."

My fists clenched at my sides. It took everything I had not to scoop her up in my arms and show her all the ways I agreed with her. But she had to do this. She had to get through this and figure out what she wanted for herself. Evie had to *choose* me.

We'd never work out otherwise, no matter what sort of possibilities might be shimmering between us.

"That's an idealist's response," Caelan said, his hands stretched toward her.

I winced.

"Power roars through your veins, Evie. All the power in the world. You owe a responsibility to your people to ensure your line runs true."

Evie tilted her head and studied Caelan, but the bond between us flared with white hot furious power. She was *pissed*. "What if we had a child who didn't meet your standards?"

Caelan blinked.

"What if we had a child who was neither Chimera, nor shifter, nor fully fae? What would you do?"

"I—" Caelan fumbled for words. "I think it depends."

"Depends on what?" Evie's voice was soft and deadly. "Would you sneak into the nursery and slit our baby's throat? Or, better yet, would you call someone like Garrett and have him do your dirty work for you?"

Caelan's jaw tightened. His non-response was response enough.

"Oh, Caelan. You long for perfection, but there is nothing perfect in this world. I am not perfect and yet you still want me because of what I represent, not for what I am."

"That is not true."

"You thought Rachel was perfect even after she almost destroyed you."

He shook his head. "No. That was Lugh's influence."

Evie took a step forward. "I know you…touched her." I heard her throat click in a dry swallow. "You did things with her. Things an engaged man should never—" Her voice thickened with tears, and she cut herself off.

I sucked in a shocked gasp. What Evie had alluded to earlier, that painful tug I'd felt in my chest. She'd smiled and laughed her way through it, but I'd known something was wrong and had wrongly assumed it had to do with Caelan's impending visit. I would *kill* him. Infidelity in shifter relationships was not uncommon, but it was normally reserved for casual relationships, not this. Not what they were to each other. For him to have done that dishonored him, but more importantly, he had dishonored and debased her in the worst of ways.

"You sonofabitch," I hissed, stepping forward.

Evie held up her hand. "No," she said softly. "This has nothing to do with you."

She hadn't yet realized this had everything to do with me.

Caelan went bone white. "*Evie.*" He stepped so close to the ward, it shimmered scarlet, a final warning to stay away.

"Simone told me," Evie said. "She walked in on you accidentally, and you were so…" Her voice breaks, taking my heart with it. "*Distracted,* you didn't even see her. If you wonder why your most loyal person abandoned you, I hope you think of that moment. But even after that betrayal, Simone hesitated to tell me because she knew it would destroy everything. Even then, there was still a thin thread of loyalty to you." Her voice shook. "I never thought you would do something so heinous, not after everything we went through. Maybe you were under Lugh's influence, but that—" She shook her head. "Not even Lugh could have made you do that if you hadn't wanted to. And here you stand, hoping to come back to me. You weren't even going to tell me."

A harsh laugh escaped her. "I know now I can never meet your needs."

Her form outlined itself in a crimson shimmer, her features morphing into a woman, smaller and curvier than Evie. Long amber hair tumbled over her shoulders in a shiny waterfall.

I froze. Rachel stood before Caelan fluffing her hair. The Lord stumbled back, swearing viciously.

Evie ran her hands over her new curves and swayed side to side. "Is this what you wish I was?" She turned her head to the side, cat-like green eyes batting her eyelashes at him. "A full shifter. A full blood. Someone who can give you lots of little pure wolf babies?"

"Don't," Caelan snarled. "This is beneath you!"

Evie snorted. "Changing into the woman you tore this all apart for is beneath me? And what about you?"

He shoved a hand through his hair, leaving it standing on end. "I—Evie, you and I were fighting, and I felt all this hatred." Caelan blew out a breath and growled. "I needed—"

The Lord couldn't form a complete sentence. "She was there, and you weren't, and I wanted the release. That's all it was."

"Oh," Evie said. "A wham, bam, thank you ma'am, then. No biggie."

A hopeful light appeared in his eyes, and he reached for that false lifeline not realizing it was a venomous snake ready to ensnare him.

You idiot.

"Yes," he breathed. "That's all. Convenience, Evie. It will never happen again. I never would have done such a thing if Lugh hadn't made me see Rachel in a different light. I hate her. I've always hated her."

"I see," Evie said. "You didn't want her. You wanted me."

"Exactly."

Rachel's form shimmered away, leaving Evie standing there. From the way she jerked, she'd forgotten she'd lose her clothes during the shift. I shrugged off my jacket and strode over, draping it over her shoulders.

"Thank you," she whispered.

"You," Caelan snarled at me. "I bet you're loving this."

What I'd love was to punch him repeatedly in his smug face. "If you think I'm loving seeing Evie's heart break, you don't know me at all."

A muscle in his jaw ticked. "This is between Evie and me. You can leave."

Evie reached out, wrapping her fingers around my forearm.

Caelan's teeth pulled away from his lips. "Is this how it is?"

"You've always seen whatever you wanted to, rather than the truth. Evie and I have always been friends. If she wants me here, I'll stay with her."

Caelan crossed his arms over his chest. "Evie. Come back to Joy Springs. Let's talk."

"I have nothing to say to you." But we both heard the tremor in her voice.

His eyes softened. "I know what I did was heinous, unforgivable even. But we can try to work through this. You and I have been through too much to walk away from each other."

"And our children?"

"We will deal with it when it happens."

I felt the moment they sundered, the second Evie let go. Underneath our feet, the earth rumbled with her anger. Magic shimmered around her body, watermelon tourmaline with hints of crimson curling through the air.

"Our children are not an *it*." Hair the color of night floated around her head, a crimson spark ringing her azure eyes.

"I didn't mean that." Caelan swallowed hard and looked to me as if I would help. "Evie, you have to believe I would love whatever children we brought into the world."

"LEAVE." Her voice was a dark command.

His jaw took on a stubborn tilt. "No."

I glanced at Evie, seeing the barely suppressed rage in her slender form, then at Caelan. "I'd do what she asks," I said softly.

"Oh, you *would* want me to leave," Caelan snapped, eyes flashing gold. "This is perfect for you."

Evie shifted in a heartbeat, into a jet-black thing of teeth and claws, and sailed through my wards.

I barked a laugh. "Told you so."

CHAPTER
Twenty

My muscles elongated, sleek and powerful. Sharp, serrated teeth formed in my mouth, sharp against my thick tongue. Claws stretched from jet-black paws, gleaming white under the moonlight. Fury drove me forward, the urge to hurt, to harm, to tear something or someone apart roaring through my blood.

A crimson sheen rolled over my eyes. Wind ruffled my sleek fur as I sailed through the air. Caelan's eyes widened. He jerked back, arms pinwheeling as he struggled to right himself.

His usual grace went under the onslaught of my speed. We collided, Caelan slamming to the ground, face up. My paws rested on either side of his head. A low snarl rumbled in my throat, but now that I had him, my anger began to slowly dissolve.

"Rowan," Caelan pleaded, lowering his eyes from mine.

He knew who the dominant one was today.

"She told you to leave," Rowan said mildly. He stepped up beside us, gliding a gentle hand over the back of my head. My fury melted away, leaving only a horrific, bone-deep sadness.

"Evie has to come back to Joy Springs. Her life is there."

He spoke about me like I wasn't standing over him. Had he ever really seen me?

Rowan stroked my fur again. "Are you able to speak, Evie?"

Garbled speech was something I was still working on, but I didn't feel like talking right now. When I did nothing, Rowan spoke once more. "She's aware of her responsibilities and will return in her own time."

Caelan lay perfectly still underneath me. I leaned in, lifting my lips to show him all my new and pretty teeth and let a slow snarl rumble through my throat.

Rowan chuckled.

Saliva dripped from my fangs, plopping onto Caelan's exposed throat.

"Will you tear my throat out, Evie?" Caelan asked quietly, his words steady despite the fear saturating his scent. "Are you that vindictive?"

"You're a fucking idiot, man," Rowan said in disbelief. "You have a predator right at your throat, close enough to your jugular to end you before you even have the chance to shift, and you're still antagonizing her." He shook his head. "Gotta say. If Evie did tear through your neck, I wouldn't feel sorry for you."

"You think you've won her?" Caelan asked.

I had to force myself not to bite him just for being an idiot.

"Evie is not a prize. Thinking that way is what led to your downfall." Rowan sounded bored, but I knew him well enough to know how furious he was.

Confusion entered his eyes. "Downfall? I do not need a Lady to cement my position as Lord."

"If that is true, why have you pursued her so relentlessly?"

"Wouldn't you?" Caelan snapped. "She has—" His eyes widened as he realized what he'd almost revealed.

"She has what?" Rowan coaxed. "Beauty? Power? All the things that might secure your shaky Lordship?"

Caelan's eyes flashed with rage.

I stilled, unsure what Rowan was talking about.

His hand came to rest on the back of my neck. "After the

disaster in Joy Springs, the Lords called an emergency meeting. Caelan here is barely hanging onto power by a thread."

"That is not why I came here." There's a desperate note in his voice. For the first time, I'm positive he's lying to me.

Stars burst behind my eyes. Holding this new form burned more magic than expected. Maybe it's because I was exhausted, both mentally and physically. Maybe it's because I was not quite a normal jaguar—the serrated teeth and overly long claws were more for shock value than practical purposes, though I'd thought long and hard about using them on Caelan—but a fine tremor began in my limbs, so subtle I know only me and possibly Rowan could sense the weakness.

Disgust filled me. With Caelan, with everything I'd been through, with everything coming up that I'd have to deal with once more. I was so tired and heartbroken, and once this was over, I wondered if I'd have to once again pick up the pieces of my life and start all over.

Rowan's fingers tightened in my ruff as I took a step back.

"Leave," Rowan commanded. "Do not return to my territory again. You know the laws as well as I do. If you come back here, you do so at your own peril."

Caelan, defiant to the end, snorted with disgust.

"Do not mistake my youth for weakness," Rowan said, his face stoic even in the face of Caelan's derision. "I knew the moment you stepped onto my territory, and you are here at my own sufferance. You mean something to Evie, and Evie is important to me."

We made our way back through Rowan's wards, and when the wards reformed, we turned to face Caelan once more.

I was having trouble walking. Shifting like this so soon after the siphoning had gone so wrong was a mistake. But I would not collapse with Caelan watching.

"Go home," Rowan said. "Evie will return in her own time."

Caelan rose, dusting the dirt and grass from his clothing. He speared me with a golden-eyed look. "She returns in three days, or I'll have her shop shut down."

I froze, resisting the urge to leap forward and bite his face off.

"Do you really think in the face of everything, that will endear you to her?"

"She exists and thrives due to my influence. Imagine what will happen if I withdraw that support." Caelan stuck his hands in his pockets. "Three days, Evie. Then we will talk without Rowan's influence."

I showed him my teeth.

Caelan smiled at me, rage glittering in his golden eyes. "There is much unsaid between us. Come home, Evangeline."

He turned and walked away, eventually fading into the heavy layer of fog that lay over Rowan's land.

Rowan exhaled. "I'm sorry, Evie." He stroked an absent-minded hand over my fur. "Come. We have things to discuss as well."

I took a step toward the house and swayed, bumping against Rowan's thigh.

He bent and scooped me into his arms, chuckling as I swatted him with a massive paw. "Pretty little deadly kitty," he cooed.

ROWAN FETCHED a robe and walked out of the kitchen to give me time to shift and dress. I'd just finished tying the sash in a knot when he knocked on the door frame, his face turned away.

"I'm decent." Not that he hadn't already seen me in all my glory more than once.

He strode in, a wary look on his face. Instead of asking me if I was alright, he went straight to one of the cabinets and pulled two rocks glasses down. "Want a drink?"

I sank into a kitchen chair. "Gods yes."

He flashed a smile and poured us both a large glug of something strong and brown. I took the glass from his outstretched fingers and tossed the entire drink down in one swallow. Rowan poured me another and brought the bottle with him to the table.

"Funny how fast a buzz can wear off when trouble arrives."

He took the seat opposite and watched me, long fingers swirling the rim of his glass.

I didn't want to talk about that. Not yet. "You shared something with me earlier."

Our eyes met. "I did."

"Is your mother still alive?"

He smiled. "She is. Mom is full fae."

A bad feeling churned in my gut. "Where is she?"

"She lives in one of the other realms."

"Rowan," I breathed. "The bridge is gone."

He nodded. "It's been a while since I've seen her."

My heart hurt for him. All those people I'd trapped over there. I might not have meant to do it, but once I'd absorbed the tree's magic, no one but the most powerful of gods and goddesses could cross over now. "Why didn't you say anything?"

He sipped his whiskey. "You have more problems to deal with than worrying whether I get to visit my mother."

"No. You are my friend and you must know I would escort her here or you there if you ever wanted to go. Dad says I'll be able to travel instantaneously soon, even without the benefit of being the bridge. I can go wherever I want, so even if I'm back in Joy Springs, I can be here almost instantly."

His face fell. "You're returning."

"We both know I have to go. Caelan will destroy my shop if I don't."

A heavy sigh escaped him. "You can rebuild here."

I smiled at him. "I know. We both knew it would come to this. I can't abandon everything forever, even if I wanted to. There are people in Joy Springs relying on me. I have land I need to tend to."

He swallowed and scratched at a nick in the table. "I understand."

Rowan was uncharacteristically silent. I took a sip and smiled at him. "I will not leave until your land is cleansed of the rot infesting it."

He glanced up in surprise. "If it takes longer than three days?"

"Have you forgotten who I am and who my daddy is? What good is all this power if I can't make a shop magically disappear?"

His laugh this time was genuine. "I hope you never use those powers for evil."

I tapped my fingers together like a criminal mastermind. "Let's see what kind of trouble I can get into in three days."

"I believe in you."

We grinned at each other until his smile slipped. "Caelan is a fool," he said softly. "You are a prize beyond gold, and he tosses you aside like yesterday's trash."

My amusement turns to ash. "I don't know what I did wrong."

Confusion glimmers in his hazel eyes. "Nothing." He shook his head with vehemence. "You did nothing wrong."

I tipped the rest of my whiskey back and tugged the bottle over, pouring us both another round. "It's not all Caelan's fault, though I appreciate how you defend me."

"Give me an example." His eyes burned with anger.

"The automaton," I said.

He waved a hand. "That was before you were an item."

"Keeping my Chimera identity secret. Claiming a piece of his land. Antagonizing the Lords. Taking and keeping Donovan's land instead of turning it over."

Rowan seems unimpressed by my list of supposed sins.

He held up a finger. "Chimera are hunted with little mercy. You kept the secret to save your life and those of your friends." Another finger. "Your power does not covet more power, Evie. It covets to heal. Return the land to him when you go back to Joy Springs. An easy enough fix." A third finger and a slow smile. "They started it."

A bark of laughter escaped me.

The fourth finger came up. "You won the land through might and power, wresting it from a greedy caretaker. If you want to return the land, you can do so at any time, but why give the Lords any more power? Keep the territory. Heal the land. You are the fae queen. They cannot wrest it back even if they tried."

"You make me sound like a redeemer rather than a tyrant."

"A tyrant?" He chuckled. "I've never seen you take a single thing for yourself. Not even a compliment." Rowan smiled to soothe the hurt of his words. "A tyrant rules without regard for law or justice."

"Would you take the land if you could?"

Rowan sat back in his chair and watched me, his face betraying nothing. "I do not seek power for power's sake, only so that I can protect my own. The land borders mine. I would not take it from anyone who holds it, but if I had done what you did to Donovan, then yes, I would have taken the land, too."

"Having Donovan's territory would strengthen your position with the Lords."

"Perhaps, but it would also make me an even larger target when one of them thinks I have too much." He tilted his head. "Why are you asking me such things?"

"I am overwhelmed," I admit. "That spell would never have reached your borders if I'd been paying attention and nourishing those lands like I do my own."

"Nonsense. How could you have known? You live thousands of miles away."

"I could have checked on the property a hundred times."

"Ninety-nine times you were dealing with Caelan, or your father, or the weight of the crown that no doubt lies heavy on your head." He tilted the glass back and drank the rest of the liquor. "There's something I need to tell you."

I rubbed my hand over my face, feeling the effects of the booze. A liquid warmth spread through my blood, lending everything a sparkling haze. "Nothing surprises me anymore. Do your worst."

He laughed and pushed the bottle over. As I poured another, he spoke. "Your father thinks I would be a good king."

My hand shook as I set the bottle down. "Does he now?" I asked quietly.

"I think he's full of shit and he's playing a long game where the rules are secret."

"Sounds about right," I muttered. "What did you tell him?"

"The same thing I've always said. You will choose your own husband and king one day. I am not the kind of male who forces myself on someone, nor do I seek more power than I already have. My people are happy and content. As such, I am happy and content."

I studied Rowan, the way the low light in the kitchen made the golden highlights in his hair stand out and the green in his eyes glow. He could not be more different than Caelan in a thousand different ways, and yet he is a Lord as well, a powerful shifter caught up in political games I never wanted to be involved in. He knows how to play his part with charm and cleverness, and yet, I am a wild animal trapped in a net, struggling to find her way out but only succeeding in entangling myself more.

Something grew between us, a fragile and sparkling thing, but I had no closure with Caelan, only hurtful words and wounds. My heart was a bruise, and I didn't think I could do this all over again, not without losing a piece of myself. I'd trusted Caelan only to be so horribly let down that even thinking of the things that passed between us hurt like a knife slid between my ribs.

"Your father did have a point," Rowan continued.

"I'm sure I'm going to love this," I muttered.

He grinned. "He thinks it's a good idea for you to claim some of my land—"

I opened my mouth to protest, but he held a hand up. "And I think it's a good idea. Doing so will help protect my territory from that goddess or witch or whoever it is responsible for this most recent chaos. You destroyed part of the spell on the edge of my border, so we know you can fight this new magic. Encircling my entire territory will keep the spell from spreading."

"Maybe," I said, the reluctance in my voice obvious. "A big if. I'm not sure my magic will stretch that far."

Rowan laughed. "You always underestimate yourself. You're the fae queen, Evie. The entire world can be yours if you want to take it from the humans or the Lords themselves."

I grimaced. "No thank you."

"The fact remains you could easily do this and maybe this is the only way to cast out the magic. See how it works with my lands, then offer to do such for the other territories. Once we find the culprit, then you can release the Lords' lands back to them."

As ideas went, this one wasn't terrible. "The other Lords covet power too much. They'd never let me take a piece even if it was done to protect them."

"Ben would. I believe Thorin would as well. Soren is fifty-fifty, but if you brought Moira in to convince him, I think he would bend."

Moira hadn't said a word about Soren in months, nor had I seen him around much. That was a story she did not want to tell, but I'd wrest it from her, eventually.

"Ethan and Caelan might be a hard pass, though if Caelan thought it would put him back into your good graces, it's possible he would relent if only to worm his way back into your life."

I shot him a dark look.

He winked. "I trust your judgment. You know him better than I do."

"I really don't. You've known him for much longer than me, and sometimes it seemed like you were the only one able to reason with either one of us." I squinted. "Why did you do that, anyway? If you felt you wanted us to be more than friends?"

Rowan's brow furrowed. "Hold on. You've always been my friend, so don't go getting spun up believing I befriended you to get us here. I did not."

I believed him. There was never a moment we'd been together where I thought he was false or using me for his own gain. When I nodded, he continued.

"All I want is your happiness. If that means being with Caelan, I will accept your decision."

I exhaled softly. "You really mean that, don't you?"

Rowan rose and swayed. I snickered when he put his hand out to steady himself. "Mom and Hazel could be billionaires if they ever sold that stuff en mass."

"I'll get the drops." He made his way over to the fridge and retrieved a small amber bottle. "You might want to bring some water to bed just in case we underdose ourselves. I've never taken this."

Rowan dispensed a few drops into his mouth before handing me the bottle.

"My mom gave you an unmarked bottle full of liquid you're supposed to consume and you just...took it?" I stared at him in disbelief.

He shrugged. "Cliona doesn't seem like the poison type. Plus, I think she likes me better than Caelan." With a wink, he tugged me from the seat and pulled me in for a hug.

I wrapped my arms around his waist and laid my head against his chest. His heartbeat was a comforting, rhythmic thud against my ear.

"Are you alright?"

I wasn't. Not by a long shot. "It's hard for me to believe everything was a lie."

His arms tightened around me. "Because it wasn't. Life is far more complicated than that. Caelan will never be a one-dimensional villain, Evie. He's not a villain at all."

I craned my head up and looked at him. "What the hell, Rowan? How are you so damned nice all the time?"

He booped my nose with a finger. "I'm nice to you. Not everyone. Caelan loves you. He has from almost the second he met you. There is a bond between you, but it is not a mating bond. He, like all shifters, has an animal side, and animals form strong bonds. Wolves gravitate toward power. His wolf approves of you and desires you to be with Caelan, but it's the man who's struggling with his doubts. Wolves do not think that far into the future. If your children turn out to be something other than wolf shifters, his animal will adapt. Caelan may not. This was never a question of him loving you. A blind man could see how he feels about you."

He tilted my chin up. "The question is, does he love you enough? Does he love you like you need to be loved? When you see yourself twenty years in the future, is Caelan the one sitting beside you?"

I was a little drunk and a little emotional, but his words still sank into my bones. Two months ago, my answer would have been of course. There were times I was unsure, but I always managed to work through those. But now, seeing him again only saddened me. My heart hurt every time he looked at me because he didn't look at me with love. He looked at me as if I belonged to him. And even now, when he obviously wanted me back, his words felt like knives against my skin.

"A man would be a fool not to want to know you. Does Caelan truly know who you are or does he only understand what drives you? A strategist knows the second. A man knows the first. There can be no doubts in your heart when you decide, Evie. You two are already on your way to something toxic, but there's still time to right the boat."

I slid my palms up Rowan's chest and stood on my tiptoes, still unable to look him in the eye unless he looked down at me. Our eyes met. "Do you want me to right the boat?" I whispered.

A ring of gold appeared around his irises. "I see so much potential in you, Evie. You have the world in your hands. But you cannot rise and become who you're meant to be while you harbor such serious doubts and mistrust. If you decide to trust Caelan, you must do so with your entire heart and soul."

"You didn't answer my question." Our lips were so close I could kiss him. "Your answer was very fae-like."

A smile curved his lips. "We have an early morning. Your

father will be here to escort Moira to the other side, and you need to rebuild your magic. I'll walk you to your room."

I thought about pressing things, but there was a look in Rowan's eyes that made me hesitate. Instead, I ran my fingers through his hair, scratching through his scalp. His eyes fluttered shut, a soft sigh parting his lips.

Leaning forward, I brushed a soft kiss over his lips and pulled away. "Good night, Rowan."

His hands tightened on my waist as if he would ask me to stay. After a moment, he let go, a rueful smile on his face. "'Night, Evie."

He did not walk me to my room.

CHAPTER
Twenty~One

MOIRA

Someone was in my bedroom. I reached under my pillow, flung the knife in the direction of the intruder, and rolled off the edge of the bed on the opposite side.

The knife landed with a meaty thunk. A soft, masculine curse rang out in the room before the voice drawled, "Do you normally attack people before you see who's come to call?"

I poked my head above the mattress and glared at Evie's dad. A thin trickle of golden blood dripped from a small wound in his chest that closed as I opened my mouth to speak. "First of all, you aren't *people*. Second, it's customary to knock on someone's door before you enter their room. What if I were naked?"

It was the wrong question to ask. Cernunnos arched an eyebrow. "Do you normally sleep naked?"

My eyes narrowed. "I am not answering that question."

To my surprise, he laughed. "Come, god touched. There are things I must show you today."

That title again. I didn't like it. Flicking my fingers to make him turn around, Cernunnos sighed and wheeled away, crossing his arms over his chest.

"Get out!" I tossed a pillow at his head.

He sucked in a surprised gasp and spun around. "Remind me

never to wake you out of a sound sleep again. You're quite cranky in the mornings."

"If you don't shut up and turn around, I'm going to throw something sharper at you."

"Sharper than your pointy little needle blade?" At my glare, he rolled his eyes and turned around. "I'm not leaving. If we walk out of here, you're going to want to eat breakfast and gab with my daughter. We're leaving right from this room."

"I need coffee."

He snapped his fingers. A steaming travel mug of coffee sat on the nightstand.

"And I have to brush my teeth."

A sink and my toothpaste and toothbrush appeared, along with the exact type of mouthwash I used. Smug bastard thought of everything. "I hate you," I muttered.

Cernunnos laughed. "Five minutes, Moira. At three, I'll start harassing you to hurry."

I rose and quickly dressed, keeping an eye out to see if he peeked. But Cernunnos was true to his word. Three minutes later, he started humming a game show theme. I brushed my teeth and ran a brush through my hair before tying it into a messy ponytail. At the one-minute mark, he stalked toward me.

I squawked and threw my shoe at him. He caught it one-handed and tossed it back. "Stop throwing things at me."

"Stop being annoying!" I snapped back. "I'm tired. The sun isn't even out!"

"The better to see the darkness with, my dear."

I glared at him. "One day I'm going to sneak into your house and wake you up the same way," I muttered.

His teeth flashed white. "You are still a pup. Good luck finding me."

"I'll just ask Evie."

He reached down and gripped me by the upper arm. "Time's up."

I snatched my coffee from the nightstand as the room sparkled with emerald and gold magic. A moment later, we were gone.

I HAD no idea where we were, but even more important than that, I was freezing my ass off. Snow littered the ground, at least six inches deep.

"Seriously? You couldn't give me a hint to dress a little more appropriately for the weather?"

To his credit, Cernunnos blushed. "I don't often think of those things." He waved a finger at me.

A heavy jacket landed on my shoulders. Waterproof, knee-high boots replaced my sneakers, and a thermal undershirt and leggings appeared underneath my jeans and hoodie.

"Better?"

"Yes, but if you have gloves and a hat, that would be better."

A second later, they appeared. "Cashmere. Nice. Evie would approve."

Cernunnos grunted. "Can you sense anything?"

"I'm not like Evie. You might have to direct me, but let me try first." I sat on the ground, relieved when Cernunnos cleared the snow so my pants wouldn't get soaked. Sticking my fingers in the ground wouldn't work for me. I was no Floromancer. My magic had always been a little odd, but after that fight where I got caught in the crossfire of some seriously heavy magic, my power had been forever altered in ways I was still trying to understand.

I couldn't make flowers grow out of thin air or heal the land or anything glorious like that, but I could suss out suspicious magic, and I was better at identifying signatures than most people I knew. Vampires possessed excellent senses, smell, hearing, taste, all of them. Once I got a taste of the magical signature causing this, I could follow the person to the ends of the earth, even if I didn't know who they were.

Surprising me, Cernunnos sat beside me. "I will guide you when you are ready."

I closed my eyes and cleared my mind. Power crackled around Evie's father like an out-of-control bonfire. He was made of magic—an ancient, cruel power far older than anyone I'd ever met. Sitting next to him felt dangerous. He was a nuke who could go off at any time, and I'd be helpless in the crossfire.

"Concentrate, god touched," Cernunnos murmured.

"Shhh," I whispered. "You're already distracting enough."

"Do you need me to move?"

"No. Just be quiet."

"Very well." He sounded offended, which almost made me laugh.

I let out a slow breath and brought my attention to my surroundings. There were mountains around us, telling me we were not in Caelan's territory. Snow, so not in Soren's. Maybe Ethan's or Thorvin's. Ben was in the Midwest. Snow, yes, mountains, not so much. Unless you counted the Ozarks, which I didn't. At least, not from the quick glance I took when I sat down.

Possibly we were still in Rowan's territory, though the air smelled different and it was a little harder to breathe. Colorado maybe?

The location didn't matter all that much. I was here to figure out who wanted to harm Danu and Evie by extension. My mind's eye scanned for rogue magic on the surface, but there was nothing. I did a deeper scan, sensing some animals in hibernation and some life flying above us. Normal things, nothing alarming, except for the supernova of magic sitting next to me.

"I'm going to need you to guide me," I murmured.

Cernunnos took my hand, jerking me along the shooting star of his magic. My consciousness was yanked out of my body and sent soaring into the ground. Holy shit. Was this what Evie experienced every time she siphoned or communed with the land?

Even with the frigid temperatures above, life bloomed beneath. Flashes of color among the darkness streaked along my peripheral vision as Cernunnos transported me to the heart of the spell.

Whoever did this was intelligent, Cernunnos admitted.

I jerked at the sound of his voice in my head. *How are you doing this?*

I had no mouth, no face, no body. How were we talking?

Did you forget me being very magical, was his dry response.

Humble, too.

His amusement floated down the link before we stopped abruptly. *There,* he said. *Can you sense it?*

A malevolent presence surrounded us, sentient and curious. *Yes. You can't get rid of it?*

I am more like Danu than others, he admitted. *Engaging will deplete my magic, and I must be prepared for other…occurrences.*

With Evie?

Concentrate, god touched, he said instead. *See what information you can obtain. We don't have much time before its curiosity wears off.*

Heeding his warning, I studied the entity as it inched closer, my mind trying to grasp knowing my body wasn't here. How could I touch something when I didn't exist? Whatever this thing was, it possessed spell components, but it wasn't completely a spell. Curious, the thing floated closer, moving similar to how an amoeba would. No arms, no legs, just a blob of magic, corrupting everything it touched. The soil around the entity died as it moved.

Cernunnos moved me back a few feet. *Hurry,* he urged.

I need to touch it.

Absolutely not.

If I don't, I'm guessing. Once I make contact, I'll be able to track this if the person responsible is close by. I know I can't physically reach out, but I can try to wrap my thoughts around it and see what I can find out.

The god hesitated. *Evie will have my hide if I risk your life.*

You aren't doing anything. I'm telling you what I need. If you take me back now, none of us will get the answers we need.

He wavered until I took the decision out of his hand. I lunged, slipping my consciousness free of his hold, and enveloped the presence.

Darkness coated my thoughts in inky night, but this presence didn't feel inherently evil to me. It simply existed, and its existence was dangerous to everything it touched.

Including me. Neither human nor animal, the presence still held a sentient, almost alien intelligence. Was it a spell that had gone wrong or was this meant to target one thing or person? I couldn't tell.

Once it got over its surprise, it wrapped itself around me, clinging like a barnacle to my consciousness, and it drank me down, stealing my thoughts and memories, rifling through them like a hacker with stolen credit card info. My magic drained, stolen away to power this thing.

MOIRA!

A shout of horror and a hard jerk on my arm, followed by a suction sound and an ominous pop, and Cernunnos and I were flying through the ether.

His grip was bruising, the fury he tried to contain burning against our link. My energy faded slowly into darkness.

Twenty-Two

"Your friend is an idiot!" Dad yelled, shoving a hand through his hair. His normal calm and cool exterior had disappeared the second he and Moira had appeared on Rowan's land, right next to me as I knelt in the bed boosting the roses I'd brought back earlier.

I had a million questions and zero time to ask them. My best friend was too pale and motionless. "Kinda busy here, Dad."

Moira lay on the ground, oblivious to the world. My hands glowed with magic, sweeping back and forth over her body, restoring function to her limbs. Whatever had done this had completely wiped her out. Her magic registered as a faint blip inside her body. Moira's organs were close to failure; her heart pumping at three times its usual rate. I closed my eyes and allowed my power to seek out the worst injuries, healing with a gentle touch as best I could.

Dad had brought her back to me close to death and couldn't save her thanks to the type of magic used. As it was, Dad's hands were disfigured and burnt from carrying her back here. I couldn't afford to tap all my power to save her, otherwise I might find myself trapped in the ground for a few days and miss Caelan's deadline. But if it came down to my shop and land and Moira's life, I'd risk it.

Rowan was on his knees beside me, in the event I needed him to hold Moira down. Sometimes when people came back from the brink, they seized, but Moira hadn't moved an inch. My friend looked dead, a thought that threatened to make me freeze in horror. The only thing keeping me moving was the soft rise and fall of her chest.

She was breathing, which meant she was alive. I allowed my magic to do one final pass before I sat back on my haunches. "I've fixed everything I could. She'll need a few days of rest and cannot use any magic, otherwise she might undo all the work I've done here."

Dad squeezed his eyes shut. I watched him carefully. His reaction seemed over the top. Even when I was injured, he kept his shit together. Why was he so beside himself with Moira?

"I'll move her to the main house," Rowan said as he got to his feet and extended his hand to help me rise.

But Dad stopped him. "No. I'll take her to the fae lands. She'll recover faster there."

I started. "Um. What? Why? She's not from there. If she's here, I can watch over her and continue with her healing."

Dad's jaw tightened, a stubborn twist to his lips as he bent to scoop her up.

"No!" I snapped, snatching his hands away. "Let me look at you before you touch her."

He sighed but held his hands out for an inspection. Touching Moira had infected him. His golden hands were blackened all the way to the wrists, his fingers cracked and blistered.

I hissed in sympathy and took both of his hands in mine. Closing my eyes, I swept over his wounds with my magic, healing all the deeper burns and blisters and cleansing his system of the spell. When I finished, I released him and scooted back. "Why can I cleanse this magic, but you can't?"

Dad shook his head. "I'm not sure. Moira got close enough to figure out what it was. When she wakes up, I'll talk to her."

Rowan walked away, a far enough distance to give us privacy. "What happened? Why are you being such a worrywart over Moira?"

Dad rolled his eyes. "She's your best friend. I would not deprive you of her presence if given a choice."

We both knew it was more than that. "Dad," I said in a warning tone.

He huffed. "She's important. That's all I will say."

I glanced down at my friend. Moira had a pale, fragile beauty, but she was anything but weak. My heart hurt for her. "Important how? To you? To the world? Is she going to end up like me?"

Dad smiled sadly. "Her exposure to the magic all those months ago has changed her in unexpected ways. Moira has a part to play in certain events."

"Shit," I said with feeling. "Does she know?"

"Moira knows more than she lets on, but no, I do not believe she knows what fate has yet in store for her."

"Can't they find someone else?" I muttered miserably.

Dad laughed, but the sound was more sad than amused. "Certain magic is useful for certain trying periods. But I will keep a close eye on your friend." He bent and scooped her into his arms.

I rose and stroked her dark hair away from her face. Moira looked vulnerable but peaceful. My heart hurt seeing her this way. "I want proof of life when she wakes up."

"I have plenty of healers on staff. With the magic gone from her system, they'll be able to help her more than you can right now."

I frowned. "Rowan tattled?"

Dad winced. "He worries for you."

"Yeah, well, Caelan is being a huge dick right now."

He made an affirmative noise but said nothing else.

"He's free of Lugh's magic, isn't he?"

His eyes softened. "Yes, Evie. I personally checked on him a few days after the incident in town."

The *incident*. Like I'd accidentally tucked my skirt into my underwear and walked out of the bathroom, and not straight up ruined my life by turning into a monster straight out of a feverish nightmare.

"Just a dick then," I said with a sigh. "Pity."

Dad adjusted Moira and touched my shoulder. "Sometimes, fate gives us blessings that look like curses. Perhaps this is one of them."

"I know what you said to Rowan."

Dad didn't even have the grace to be embarrassed. "What of it?"

"Stop playing matchmaker, you interfering hen!"

He snorted. "Rowan would make a good king."

"And?"

"And every good queen needs a good king by her side."

"Same for kings?"

His eyes narrowed as he realized the trap I'd set for him. "Evie—"

"Seems like you need a good queen, but I don't see anyone applying for the job. Maybe I should put an online ad out, or better yet, sign you up for online dating. Do you know how many people would throw themselves at the chance to date the Fae King?"

"Former," Dad growled. "Very funny, Evie. I do not need your help to find someone."

"Check and mate," I said. "I'm not sure what's going to happen, but I do not need you to find me a king or a boyfriend. Caelan might not be working out, but that doesn't mean I want another boyfriend or fiancé right away."

Dad's eyebrows lifted. "Could have fooled me. You and Rowan have unfinished business."

I crossed my arms over my chest. "Go away. Bring her home by tomorrow."

"I'll bring her home when she's better and not a minute beforehand."

"Don't make me come get her." A thought occurred to me, but I held my tongue. I'd only prove his point if I asked him the question. Mom would be here for lunch. I'd ask her instead.

He dropped a kiss on top of my head. "I want you to be successful, Evangeline. But I also want you to experience healthy love. You're right about me choosing someone to spend my life with, but I do not have the freedom you do."

"I'm queen now. Aren't you free as a bird?"

Dad chuckled. "Not quite." Magic prickled my skin. "I'll try to do better," he promised as he and Moira disappeared in a shower of emerald and gold sparkles.

Rowan walked over. "I'm surprised he took her."

"Me too." I glanced up at the handsome Lord. My traitorous heart skipped a beat. He smelled wild, the scent of the PNW made flesh. His hair was mussed and a faint five o'clock shadow traced his jaw. His hazel eyes always looked greener when we were outside, and those eyes pinned me where I stood.

"Everything okay?" he asked when I didn't drop my gaze.

"Just wondering how you don't have women beating down the Keep doors 'cuz you're so pretty."

My words took him by surprise. He blinked, then burst out laughing.

"Dad says every good queen needs a king, but the same goes for him. You've never thought about taking someone as your Lady?"

The amusement in his eyes didn't fade as I expected. "Being Lady is not an easy job. Haven't you noticed all the other Lords are single?"

I had. "Isn't that because they're all assholes and players, though?"

His laugh skims over my skin, bright and wicked. "Partially," he admits. "Except for your Ben."

"Ben doesn't like it when my crazy comes out. We never

would have worked. He'll end up finding a nurturer, someone content to be led. Most people are followers, you know?"

He nodded. "It's not always easier to be a follower. Being such takes great faith in another person."

"I've never been a great follower," I admitted. "Not a great leader, either. I do it sometimes because I have to, but I'd rather be left alone."

"Yes," Rowan said, pulling me in for a one-armed hug. "Our own female Ron Swanson over here."

I gasped. "You like Parks and Rec, too?"

He laid a hand over his heart. "Best show ever."

"It's my comfort show. There's not a lot of time to watch television these days, but when I do have time, it's my favorite to watch. There's something so comforting about low stakes shenanigans and a close found family like they have."

Rowan watched me for a moment before tugging me toward the western side of his Keep. "Come. I'd like you to meet some people."

CHAPTER
Twenty~Three
ROWAN

I had Evie for only forty-eight more hours, sixteen of those soon lost to sleep. We stood inside one of the multiple dormitories hosting the shifters who didn't want to live outside the Keep.

Hope, my Omega, blinked in surprise when she spotted me standing inside the Great Room with Evie. At my request, she'd kept her distance, but since Evie had questioned why she hadn't yet met my people, I thought it might be time to introduce her to a few of my closest friends.

"Evie, this is my Omega, Hope."

She was tall and willowy, had a massive amount of curly ginger hair springing about her head like an out-of-control jack-in-the-box, and green eyes the color of a jadeite stone. I'd met her over twenty years ago when she wandered onto my lands, disoriented and wounded. Right away, I knew what she was, but I allowed her to heal and recover emotionally before I offered her a permanent home. Even after all these years, she was still recovering and would carry the reminder of what happened to her on the side of her face for all eternity. Sometimes wounds were too grievous to fully recover from, even for shifters. If she were human, her wounds would have been mortal. As it was, a thin white scar ran from the top of her left temple, crossed her cheek, and stopped at the corner of her lips. I'd called my best healers over the years, and none had been able to erase the evidence of her attack.

Evie stepped up and held her hand out. "Pleasure to meet you. Do you know Simone?"

My Omega grinned. "Everyone knows Simone and her ever-trusty tablet," she drawled as they shook hands. "I'm happy to finally meet you. Our illustrious leader has told us a lot about you, and we've heard a lot of things through the grapevine."

Evie grimaced. "Including the most recent shenanigans?"

"Oh yes," Hope said. "You had us all quivering in our boots."

Evie blinked at Hope's droll tone, gauging whether the Omega was serious before bursting into a laugh. "You aren't terrified of me?"

Hope snickered. "Should we be?"

Evie laid a hand over her chest and blinked a few times, a suspicious wetness in her eyes. "No. Never," she said vehemently.

Hope's lips parted. "Oh no. I was kidding about being terri-fied. I promise we aren't. Rowan never would have brought you onto Keep grounds if you were a threat."

Evie shook her head. "I'm happy to meet someone who doesn't automatically believe I'm a monster."

Hope's eyes softened. "Why would I? I'm well aware of what I see when I look in the mirror every day even though I know I am more than the sum of my parts. It helps having people around who don't let you sink too far into the quagmire."

Evie lifted her hand, her fingers trembling. I went still, and Hope's brow furrowed. "I—I know we just met, and I don't know your story, and I'm probably overstepping, but I have a..." She sighed. "I hesitate to call it a gift because it could very well get me killed one day, but I can heal things even powerful healers cannot. I'm due back to Joy Springs in a few days, but if you want, and if Rowan approves, I can come back and we can see about that scar. The only reason I'm asking is because many scars have underlying issues, and you might still feel pain from the wound you sustained. I can help address those issues and force even the oldest injuries to heal like they should have in the beginning."

Hope swallowed, tears filling her eyes. She brushed her fingers over her cheek. "No one has been able to erase this. And you're right, I still have pain in my jaw every time I eat."

Grief filled me. She'd never said a word, and I never noticed. What kind of leader was I to have left her in pain all these years?

"I can't make any promises," Evie said, "but the Lord of Texas and his former Second are smooth as a baby's bottom after I got a hold of them."

Hope let out a wet laugh. She looked at me. I tilted my head. My Omega knew she didn't need my permission. She'd always struggled with her appearance and rarely left the Keep unless it was for official business. Hope had yet to understand her scars did not define her. There were many men here who'd fallen head over heels for her and were merely waiting for a signal from her. But Hope saw the evidence in the mirror every day and still thought she wasn't good enough.

"Before you say anything," Evie added, "I hope you're not claustrophobic. You might have to spend some time in the dirt with me."

Hope grinned. "Good thing I like the dirt." She squared her shoulders. "Let me think about this, okay? I've worn these scars for so long I'm not sure what I'd do without them."

She'd never shown me the others, though I could only assume if the one on her face was still there, she had others on her body.

"Of course. And I'm sorry if I overstepped or overwhelmed you. You're a total hot tamale just the way you are, so I don't want you to think anything other than this as a sincere offer. I'm more concerned about the pain you must be in." Evie smiled. "And if you decide to keep your scars, I can still help with the pain."

Hope's eyes widened. "I think we're going to be the best of friends, Miss Quinn."

Evie smiled back. "I certainly hope so."

A giant of a man walked out from the back, his eyes trained on Hope.

"Declan," I said to my Second. "This is Evie Quinn."

Evie went still. Seeing Declan in the flesh gave most people pause. Where most shifters were lean but muscled, Declan looked like a grizzly in human form. He was close to seven-foot tall, tipped two hundred and eighty pounds, and had arms like tree trunks, though I'd never seen the man lift a gym weight in his entire life.

If he never spoke, you'd automatically discard him as a gym rat. Women found him unbearably handsome, and I'd had to turn many heartbroken girls away at the front of the Keep when he refused to go out with them. But he wasn't a use 'em and lose 'em kind of guy. Like me, he rarely dated, and when he did, I'd never seen him go out for more than two dates with the same woman.

The reason stood right in front of us grinning like a fiend at Evie.

Declan inclined his head. "It's a pleasure, ma'am."

Evie's lips twitched. "Just Evie, but if you see my mother around, you should definitely call her ma'am. She loves it."

Declan chuckled. "I've seen her. You favor her."

"I do."

"I'm Rowan's Second if he hasn't already told you. I hear you stole Garrett and Simone right out from under Caelan's nose."

To my surprise, Evie laughed. "Not quite. Certain events brought them to me, but I'm happy to have them."

"I've never heard of a shifter being blood sworn to a fae. How does that work?"

Evie rolled her eyes. "They take advantage of it," she said with a laugh. "I'm not the kind of person who will yank on the bond. The only order I've given them is to defend my family because I had to give one to make the oath. Let's just say they are both experts at interpreting things how they see fit."

Declan grinned. "Sounds like Garrett, that old bastard. He's got a girl with him, doesn't he? Another fae?"

"My sister. She's under his protection." For now, she didn't say. With the broken oath, Thalia's status was still up in the air. She made herself scarce with Cernunnos coming around, but she'd made no moves to leave Garrett and return to Caelan.

Not that Garrett would let her if she tried. The man had it bad for her.

Declan tipped his head to me. "I'm running out for a bit. I take it coming back into the main house is okay now that we've met Miss Evie?"

Evie frowned. "You could have come by at any time."

Declan laughed. "No Miss Evie. Not if I wanted to keep my head on my shoulders."

He bumped me with his elbow and grinned as he passed. Asshole.

I gave Evie a sheepish smile.

"You haven't met Simone yet?" Evie asked Hope after she'd rolled her eyes at me.

"Not yet. Simone is wise not to explore the Keep without Rowan. She's not tied to a Pack, and other shifters get weird about unattached paranormals on Keep grounds. Same with Garrett."

"I'll talk to Rowan tonight about bringing her over."

Hope and Evie chatted for a little while longer before my Omega excused herself, but not without giving me a long look as she walked away.

I swear. My people could be like mother hens sometimes.

"Ready to go?" I asked Evie. My chest felt warm with pride. Declan and Hope liked Evie. I found the Floromancer irresistible, but if my Pack didn't agree, we'd find ourselves in the same position as Caelan and Evie were, something I couldn't abide by.

She nodded and took my proffered elbow.

I tried not to think about her telling them she would return to Joy Springs. There was still time to change her mind. I had to believe that.

Twenty~Four

We'd just finished dinner when the phone rang, signaling a video call. I picked up immediately and saw Moira's wan face smiling at me.

"Thank the gods," I whispered. "How are you feeling?"

"Like someone beat me with a tree trunk," she admitted. "But your daddy has some good healers in his fancy little castle. They're taking good care of me. I'll be home tomorrow, no matter what he says."

"If you're still feeling poorly, just stay another day."

"Absolutely not." Her hair slid against her face like a waterfall. "My magic is drained and slow to refill this time, but I won't let you return to Joy Springs without me." She leaned the phone against something on the nightstand and shifted so she could lie down.

Moira yawned. "Listen, I have some information. You're looking for a witch, but the spell was mixed with fae DNA or magic or something." She shook her head. "Definitely fae, definitely powerful. I'm not familiar enough with your people to distinguish between male or female, but whoever this is, they're old. When we get back tomorrow, maybe we can have your dad take us hunting." She shrugged. "Or your mom. Daddy Dearest is a little intense, so I could use some girl time."

I snorted. "Did he tell you why he was being so fussy?"

Moira waved a hand in dismissal. "Something about being needed for something important. He has no idea that I'm way too tired to save the world. Plus, the world hasn't done right by me enough to care about it all that much."

"Aww, Moira." Her words saddened me.

The vampire grinned. "I'm not the only one on this planet with magic, so I don't really believe I'm set to be its savior or anything. Since he refuses to elaborate, I'm just going to let things play out and see what happens."

"You're sure the magic is a spell?"

Moira shook her head. "Not quite. It's a spell wrapped in raw magic, so it holds an odd sentience, but I can't figure out its purpose other than to destroy whatever it touches. I didn't find it to be evil. We're dealing with something that just is, if that makes any sense."

Not really, but I nodded instead. "We'll discuss it when you get back. For now, you look like you're about to fall asleep in the middle of a sentence. Let's chat tomorrow. I'll call Mom and see if she's busy."

She blew me a kiss. "Night, bestie."

"Night Moira."

We disconnected just as Rowan set a bowl of ice cream covered in hot fudge in front of me. "Oh my gosh. It's freezing outside!"

"So?" Rowan plopped into a seat and dug in. "It's never too cold for ice cream."

"Umm. Spoken like a bear."

He chuckled. "There's whipped cream in the fridge if you want some."

"Hell yes, I want some." I snagged it and added an enormous dollop. "Want some?" I waved the can at him.

He pushed his bowl toward me. "Not as much as you, whipped-cream fiend."

"The world can never have enough of this dairy delight."

We stopped talking and enjoyed our treat. When we finished, Rowan looked at me thoughtfully. "You don't have to go back, you know."

"You don't have to live alone like a Victorian widow, either. Have Hope and Declan move in and liven the place up."

Rowan burst out laughing. "Declan would throw himself out of a window if I asked him to take one of the main rooms. He likes living in a house with all those other heathens."

"And Hope?"

He shrugged. "She's still dealing with things." Rowan pushed his bowl away. "Your offer was kind. I don't know if she'll take you up on it, but to know the possibility exists…she will give the decision the weight it deserves."

"It's not your story to tell, I know, but I know she will have all the solace she needs here. I don't know what happened to her, but I suspect, and I—" I swallowed hard. "I know how it feels to pick up those pieces and try to put a damaged puzzle back together."

Rowan went completely still. "Evie?"

"Just tell her if she ever needs a friend, she can call me. No matter where I am."

He nodded. "I will tell her."

"I'm going to make a few phone calls. Mom will be here tomorrow around lunch. Are you good with getting up early to go out and check the rest of your property?"

"Six good?"

We agreed on the time, and I went to the back, ignoring the way his eyes softened when he looked at me. I was about to leave and knew I wouldn't go if I let myself feel the things my heart wanted to.

Ash's handsome face swam into view. "Evie! It's so good to see you."

"Everything good there?"

Ash's lips twisted. "No one is actively trying to sabotage us, so that's a positive. I suspect your father had something to do with that."

I winced. "I'm sorry. I'll be back in a couple of days. There's a lot we need to discuss."

"Caelan summoned us to his Keep."

I froze, anger boiling in my blood. "He did what?"

Ash nodded. "We're fine, but he's given us notice to vacate the shop premises within sixty days unless, and this is a direct quote, 'Evie comes to her senses.' I told them how insane that was, but Caelan doesn't seem like he's in a listening mood these days."

"That sonofabitch," I snarled. "He can't do that! We have a lease!"

Ash looked down and grabbed something. He held up a piece of paper and waved it at the screen. "He can and he did. There's a clause in the lease he dubbed as the Lord's clause, which to be frank, makes him sound like a giant douchebag, but it basically says he can do what he wants whenever he wants. No one in town is safe if he decides he wants their space."

"What a shit," I hissed. But as I say it, a plan began unfurling in my mind. One that would make him furious, no doubt, but it would prove my point.

"I know that look," Ash said. "Do I want to know?"

"Plausible deniability."

"Let me guess. Evie is not going to—" he makes air quotes, "—come to her senses?"

I laughed. "Not in the way he wants me to," I assured him. "When I get back, let's sit down and come up with a contingency plan. There's a lot I need to tell you."

"Sure thing, boss. How's everything going there?"

I filled him in on what was happening and what we were doing about it. When I finished, Ash had a deep frown on his face. "I'm going to call my uncle and see if he's heard of anything like this. I'll be in touch if he has. In the meantime, be careful, especially when you're in the fae lands. You may be the queen, but not everyone is happy about it."

"Will do. Very few things I do these days make anyone happy, so I guess I'll have to get used to annoying people."

We said our goodbyes, and I kicked off my shoes and curled up in the seat by the window. Rowan's land really was spectacular, even during the winter. If I didn't need to save magic, I'd go outside and explore more. Tomorrow might be a heavy magic day, and I'd be foolish to expend any more than I had to, so tonight I was safest going to bed early and being fresh as a daisy tomorrow.

———

Rowan knocked on my door at six fifteen. When I opened the door, he didn't say a word, only shoved a steaming mug of coffee and a pastry at me.

Then he walked off like I was a rabid dog, making me laugh.

"I'll be in the kitchen waiting for you. Take your time."

True to his word, he sat at the kitchen table reading the newspaper. I had no idea they made those anymore, but he had the finance pages open, reading a long column of numbers that looked like nonsense to me.

I topped off my coffee and brought the pot over to do the same for him. He gave me a distracted smile and went back to his reading, so I took the time to clear my head and get a little more caffeine in my system. That's what Mom should do. She'd be a damned trillionaire if she figured out how a paranormal could keep a caffeine buzz for longer than a few minutes.

Rowan neatly folded the paper and picked up his mug. "Need a heavier jacket?"

He eyed my bulky cashmere sweater.

"It's warm," I promised as I wiggled my fingers. "Plus, I'm wearing gloves."

He snagged his jacket and a blanket off the hook. "We don't

need to travel very far today, but it's colder outside in the mornings. Better safe than sorry."

I followed the Lord outside. We walked in silence for a while until he stopped beside a copse of trees with a large bench in the middle.

"I take my coffee out here in the spring sometimes," he said. "I'll wait here while you do your thing. Then we can get breakfast in town since you're leaving tomorrow. Sound good?"

His smile didn't reach his eyes. Rowan knew I wouldn't change my mind about returning, and this was his way of trying to deal with the decision. Caelan would never be his first choice for me.

"Of course," I said. "I'd love to go to breakfast."

The smile he gave me next was genuine. I wiped away a light dusting of snow and sat down, settling myself onto the ground. Rowan spread a blanket over my shoulders and took his spot on the bench. I shifted and looked over my shoulder. "Are you sure you're okay with this? I'll have to keep a hold on the land until the threat is gone."

"Make your mark on my territory, Evie." He winked at me and crossed an ankle over his knee.

I snorted and shook my head. "I'm serious. You're the only Lord that would allow this, you know."

"Because I trust you."

I eyed him. There was something I'd been wanting to ask him for a while now. My conversation with Ash only solidified my decision. He was the only one I'd trust with such a thing. "What would you think about taking over Donovan's territory?"

Rowan stilled. "Why would I do such a thing?"

"Because I'd give it to you."

Rowan barked a laugh. "You can't be serious."

"Why not? I trust you too. You're one of the only Lords I know who isn't mad with power."

A ring of gold outlined his irises. "Doing this would make me the most powerful Lord. You'd cement yourself to my side politically. You would forever ruin your relationship with Caelan."

My lips twisted. "I don't see that getting any better, so I don't see why it matters."

Rowan's eyes narrowed. "You aren't returning to Joy Springs for him?"

I blinked and started laughing. "Did you see how we ended things? There's probably no coming back from that."

"He asked you to come home and you said yes. What was I supposed to think?"

"Well, that I'm not an idiot would be nice. Plus, even if I had been thinking of getting back together with him, he gave us sixty days to vacate our storefront."

Rowan's eyes flared bright gold. "That sonofabitch. Don't you have a lease?"

"I do. The lease has a 'Lord clause.' He can kick us out whenever he wants for whatever reason. I assume he believes giving us sixty days is generous."

"He has a caveat, doesn't he?" Rowan sipped his mug, his eyes still glowing.

"He'll drop the eviction notice if I come to my senses. His words, not mine."

Rowan burst out laughing. "Totally reasonable request."

"He's always been a reasonable man," I said. We grinned at each other. "So what do you say? Interested in being the brand-new Lord of a shit ton of extra territory?"

He held up a finger. "I'm texting Hope and Declan. Major decisions like this require more input than just me."

Rowan's phone beeped twice in rapid succession. "Hope asked me if I was an idiot and told me I should force you into marriage immediately."

A laugh escaped me. Rowan lifted his head and wiggled his eyebrows before looking back down at his phone. "Declan said, 'Hell yes. PNW rules, other Lords drool.' As you can see, my Omega and Second are mature and reasonable adults."

"Sounds like it." Garrett and Simone rarely joked around. Was it their personalities or had serving in Caelan's Keep molded their personalities? "Now that you have their opinions, what do you think?"

Rowan set his phone down and came to sit beside me. He made no move to touch me. "You're placing a great deal of trust in me."

"You didn't shun me when you found out what I was. Instead, you welcomed me into your sanctuary and gave me choices. Your people obviously love you. If I were going to give the territory to anyone, why wouldn't it be you?"

"You're forgetting about the wannabe Lord sniffing around."

I wrinkled my nose. I'd almost forgotten about the young and unproven shifter vying for Donovan's old territory. He'd come around asking questions some time ago, and the last I heard, the Lords were considering adding him to the Council. Hard to do with my claim on the land, but they probably had a plan for that, too. "Dario? He seems more suited to a teen vampire drama than the world of the Lords."

Rowan barked a laugh. "I never thought of it that way, but you're right. He does have that look about him. Dario has enough power to become a Lord, but whether he has the stomach for it is an entirely different question. If you decide to do this, you will make an enemy of him."

"What's new? All the Lords have been a thorn in my side since the beginning. Dario is only one more to add to my list."

"I do not want the territory."

I stared at him for a moment. "Alright. Should I relinquish the lands and let the Lords fight over it?"

His expression grew somber. "I don't want it," he repeated, "but I will share it. With you. But doing so will send a message. We will be inextricably linked."

"Do you or your people have an issue with a link to a Chimera?"

A sad smile. "No. If we share the land, they won't be able to offer the territory to Dario or anyone else, but you will still be able to wrest control away from me."

"Just in case you become mad with power?"

Rowan didn't smile. "In case you decide you no longer want to associate with me."

I blinked. "Why would I do that?"

He shrugged. "Did you ever think such would happen with Caelan?"

I frowned at him, but he was right. "Fair enough. I agree to your terms, Lord Rowan."

We shook on the deal. "What's next?" he asked.

"I'll need to double-check for evidence of the spell first on both your territory and mine. Once I cleanse the land, then I'll take your hand and share the link with you. I've never done something like that, but I know how to bond with the earth. Should be simple."

Rowan's eyebrows lifted. "What if something goes wrong?"

"I always figure things out, don't I?" On that slightly ominous note, I grinned and closed my eyes. Rowan shifted closer to me, the edge of his thigh touching mine.

Once my gloves were off, I sank my fingers into the dirt, sending magic deep into the earth. Rowan had more faith in me than I did, but as I spread my magic farther and farther, I realized he was right to believe in me. Magic spiraled from my fingertips, so much I felt I could encircle the world if I needed to. I'd never needed to examine so much land before, so I'd never tried spreading my wings like this. I felt amazing.

Life bloomed under the earth, creepy-crawly things ventured closer, drawn by my power, long-extinct roots came back to life, reaching for the magic, flowers bloomed all around me and Rowan, the heady scent of honeysuckle and jasmine tickling my nose.

Rowan drew in a shocked gasp as I kept spooling my magic outward, cleansing his land of any corruption I found. And there were spots here and there, some linked to the spell's influence, some not. His land was old, much of it untouched by the current generation of humans. Spots of old fae magic lingered, so I cleansed those as well.

A laugh bubbled from my throat at the power flooding my veins like the finest champagne. Was this how I'd always been meant to use my magic? Had I unintentionally amputated my power by being so diligent about sticking to my own lands? As I worked, I realized I had the ability to purify the world if I so chose. I could bring back extinct plants and animals. My magic brushed over the long-forgotten remains of an enormous mammoth and a saber-toothed cat, and I knew in a few brushes of power, I could bring those animals back, give them another chance at life.

Resisting the urge to act as a god, I left those alone but couldn't resist healing damaged seeds of rare and long-forgotten flowers, encouraging the growth of Columbia yellowcress and a few others. Smiling as I moved closer to the edges of his territory, I healed and cleansed a particularly stubborn piece of that spell, frowning when I realized how large it had gotten.

Magic like this was insidious. If allowed to continue unchecked, the Lords would be helpless to prevent its corruption.

A few other spots and a double check, and Rowan's land was clear. I sent my power into the Great Plains area, seeking to heal and solidify my claim. The corruption was much worse on the other side of the border close to Thorvin's territory. I cleansed my side and left his alone.

He was savvy enough to sense our presence last time we intruded on his territory, and I wouldn't risk causing trouble for Rowan. He'd already stuck his neck out for me now that everyone knew what I was.

Once I triple checked for traces of old and corrupt magic, I reached out. Rowan's fingers slid through mine, callouses brushing against my palms.

"Do not be afraid," I murmured.

Rowan's fingers tightened at the words. My voice did not

sound like my own. I was deep into my power now, ancient magic crackling in my veins like wildfire. Danu's presence surrounded me, though the goddess did not intrude in my mission.

"Evie?" Concern deepened his voice.

"Thank you for your faith in me. Do not be afraid," I said again as I dropped into my full power.

A shout of alarm tore from Rowan's throat as magic roared through both of us. I'd felt many kinds of magic before, dark and light, but Floromancy felt like sitting in a field of wildflowers on a cool spring day with the sun at your back. This was the magic of the world, the beating heartbeat of the earth, this was *mine*. Rowan's gentler fae magic mixed with my own, allowing me to soak the territory with our mingled power. Just at the edge, close to Caelan's territory, I noticed an encroachment, someone trying to slowly make his mark on the land.

Dario.

With a joyful laugh, I ripped that piece of his power out and sent it sailing back into Caelan's territory, careful to stay right at the border. Once Dario's mark was gone, I poured more and more power into the earth, moving along the edges of all the borders to include Rowan's territory.

"More," Rowan murmured. "You're doing something to my land. Something good. Claim more."

I hesitated, not wanting to do something he might regret later. "Rowan…"

"Trust goes both ways."

I spread my power deeper into his borders, ensuring our link stayed strong so as not to wrest his territory away. Snow melted as the temperature rose and flowers bloomed everywhere I touched. Birds sang in the sky, and a gentle mist of rain fell onto our shoulders. That glowing golden thread between Rowan and me resurfaced, this time wrapping around both of us, a bright sparkling thing of joy.

Rowan sucked in a breath. "Evie—"

Sunk deep into the glorious magic of my ancestors, I

welcomed that thread, knowing it was good, and allowed it to soak deep into my blood and bones. My neck arched as Rowan's magic explored my very soul. Rowan's heartfelt groan of pleasure next to me told me he was experiencing much of the same thing. That spot in my chest warmed, golden light suffusing our beings with light and magic.

I'm not sure how long we sat there, but when my power was exhausted and Rowan and I now shared thousands of miles of territory, I opened my eyes only to see a botanical wonderland.

Hundreds of wolves and other creatures lay prone in a sea of multi-colored flowers and vines, glowing eyes watching us.

I started, but Rowan's hand in mine reassured me. He let out a shaky breath and ran trembling fingers through his hair. "I've never felt anything like that in my entire life," he said quietly. "We will need to speak later." Rowan looked at me, eyes widening. "Your eyes," he whispered.

I was a little magic drunk. His words registered, but I needed to sit there for a little while to let my magic settle. Getting up was out of the equation as I was covered in flowers and still flooded with power. Smiling, I lifted my hands. Trees sprang from the earth, away from Rowan's shifters, and bloomed, sending a shower of falling blossoms all around.

Rowan rose and reached for my hand. I let him pull me to my feet. When I swayed, he wrapped a firm hand around my waist. His people remained quiet and watchful.

"Everything okay?" I slurred.

Rowan let out a slow breath. "They're curious about you. People all over the world will feel what you've done here today."

I glanced at him. "I stayed within the boundaries of our territory."

His eyes glowed at the word *our*. "I know, but it doesn't matter. You've created a full spring in a land of winter. This won't go unnoticed."

"Can you walk?"

I took a step and wobbled like a newborn deer. Rowan chuckled and swept me into his arms. "Come. Let's eat."

Food sounded amazing. I patted his cheek. "You always know how to charm a girl."

To my surprise, every shifter rose when Rowan turned and followed behind, all the way to Rowan's main residence.

"Is this normal?" I whispered.

Rowan snorted. "Nothing you've done since you got involved with us has been normal."

He deposited me into a kitchen chair and rummaged through the fridge. A few minutes later, he set an enormous sandwich and a glass of water in front of me. "This should tide you over until we can get to town."

He cast a critical eye over my still wobbling body. "If you're still up for it."

I took a huge bite of the sandwich and mumbled I was. Rowan chuckled and ruffled my hair. "Good. I'll be right back."

I heard his words but was too into my sandwich for them to register.

Twenty~Five

ROWAN

Hope and Declan shifted as soon as I stepped outside. I held one finger to my lips and jerked my head for them to follow. When we were out of hearing distance, Declan spoke. I rarely saw the man disheveled, but Declan's eyes were wide, and his tan skin was pale.

"What the fuck just happened?"

Hope was slightly less freaked out. She wore a dazed and happy expression. "That. Was. Awesome! Everyone feels like they've been tripping balls for the last two hours!"

I stared at her for a long moment, realizing just how much Evie had done.

Declan shot her a quelling look. "This is serious, Hope." My Second's mouth dropped open as he did a double take.

Hope was too hyped up to notice. "Dude. I know as well as you do, but you can't deny you've never felt better, right?"

That was the clincher. Evie had shared her claim on my land and restored her claim on Donovan's old territory while also allowing me authority, but she'd also healed the land, and not quite in the way she thought she might have. All my old aches and pains were gone. Old injuries, that odd spot in my knee that twinged when rain was coming, the strange ache in the back of my neck when I slept wrong, all things shifter physiology should have fixed but didn't were now erased as if they'd never been.

Including Hope's scar.

Declan kept staring at Hope, a completely freaked out expression on his face until she finally noticed. "Dude. What?"

He opened his mouth and snapped it shut just as fast, before looking over at me helplessly.

"Declan?" Hope looked back and forth between us.

I gave her what I hoped was a reassuring smile and took her by the elbow, leading her away from the kitchen and into the laundry room area where there was a guest bathroom. After I flipped on the light, I stepped out of the way and gestured for her to go inside, waiting until she was inside before shutting the door.

Declan crossed his arms over his massive chest, his face stricken. "What the hell is she, boss?"

He wasn't talking about Hope. "She's the child of two gods and a being of mixed Chimera blood. You know she's the Fae Queen."

He nodded. "With that much power, she could be queen of the entire damned world, and I'm not sure anyone could stand against her."

Soft sobbing came from behind the closed door.

Declan's expression turned stricken. He went to go to her, but I held him back. "Wait," I said quietly. "Give her the space she needs. When she's ready, she will come out."

He blew out a frustrated breath. "I feel like I'm twenty again. Gods." He craned his neck to look up at the ceiling. "Half of the guys out there are scared shitless of her. The other half are in love with her."

Considering what Evie had done out there, I wasn't surprised. "And you?"

He ran a hand through his hair and speared me with a look. "I think you've stepped into a different world, boss, and you're taking us along for the ride. She seems like a good woman, but I've never seen so much power contained in a single person." His eyes narrowed, before widening a hair. "Oh, man," he chuckled. "You crazy sonofabitch. Does she know?"

"I don't think so." How the hell was I going to explain what she'd done and the ramifications? Part of me felt remorse. I don't think she knew exactly what she was doing when she was doing it, so wrapped in her power, she took whatever the land offered her. The other part felt a bone deep sense of rightness, of satisfaction, of knowing this was what I'd been seeking for my entire life, and she'd given it to me on a golden platter.

"Poor bastard." Declan clicked his tongue. "You know you've probably set us on a path to war with all the other Lords." He chuckled and clapped a hand over my shoulder. "Good thing you have all the territory in the world to plan your strategy now."

The bonds tugged inside my chest. I'd have to visit the new territory soon, see how I could stake a physical claim on it so the other Lords wouldn't keep trying to encroach.

Hope stepped out of the bathroom, eyes puffy and nose red. "Where is she?"

I stilled.

"Where's Evie?" Hope looked to Declan.

He held out an arm. "I'll show you."

Evie was still sitting in the kitchen when we walked in. She smiled at Hope when she saw her, but the happy smile slid off her face. "Oh. Oh gods, Hope. I am so so—"

My Omega bent and slammed into Evie, wrapping her arms around the smaller woman and burying her face into the crook of her shoulder. Sobs racked Hope's body. "Thank you. Thank you. Thank you."

Evie's wide eyes met mine. She blinked a few times and drew Hope in closer. "I did not mean to take the choice away from you."

"I don't know that I would have made it," Hope sobbed. "All I wanted for so long was to be rid of the evidence of what he'd done to me. Looking in the mirror every day told the story of my pain, but there was nothing I could do. I'd tried everything."

"This won't make the pain go away," Evie said softly.

"Yes," Hope agreed. "My physical pain is gone, which will help me put those memories to rest. It helps knowing everyone else around me won't be reminded of it as well. When I look in the mirror now, I can see me again." She rose and wiped her eyes. "If there is ever anything I can do for you, name it. You will always have a loyal friend in me."

Tears swelled in Evie's eyes. Her lower lip trembled. "I am glad I could help, even if it was done inadvertently. Again, I apologize for taking your choice away. Please know it was not my intention. Sometimes the magic sees something to heal and goes rogue."

Hope smiled. "Healing is never a bad thing." She laid her hand over her heart and bowed her head to Evie. When she turned around, both of her eyebrows lifted, and a question sparkled in her eyes. I shooed her and Declan away and sat at the table facing Evie.

"Are you alright?"

"Better. The sandwich helped. Thank you." She cringed as she looked out the kitchen window and saw all my shifters still outside waiting. "Did I do something to them? Besides a spontaneous healing?"

"They're fine. Mostly curious."

She rose and went to the kitchen window. In a small voice, she said, "Some of them are frightened, aren't they?"

Evie touched a spot in her chest. "I can feel them. In here." She exhaled a deep breath. "I should probably be more concerned about that than I am. I feel good. Better than good. There's something about this land, Rowan. It speaks to my soul."

I rose and came up behind her. My heart was both sore and full. She'd gone through so much to keep her autonomy, and this was the opposite of what she'd fought for. How could I tell her? Did I even need to?

"Do you know what happened out there?"

Her fingers tightened as she clutched the edge of the sink.

"We're bonded, you and I, aren't we? Started in the dirt a few days ago, and I solidified it earlier."

I moved closer and wrapped my arms around her. My chin rested on top of her head. Evie's hair smelled like an English garden. "The bond isn't finished."

Evie went still in my arms, whether in relief or confusion, I couldn't tell. Our bond was a lovely, soothing thing, but there was still one more step to take until we were bound permanently. Whether she would do so remained to be seen. "It feels complete."

"We are also sharing land, and we are both fae. Our bond might be different."

"Then how can you know it's not complete?"

My laugh ruffled her hair. "You will know when it's complete, Evie. I already feel you inside me, your power and your goodness, but when the bond is finished, you will be able to find me, no matter where I am."

"Do you want this?" Her voice sounded small.

I gently turned her around, trapping her against the sink in the circle of my arms. She lifted her face to mine. "More than anything in the world," I said. My heart felt tender and raw. If she wanted to wound me, she'd reject me, toss me away, and forfeit our bond. She still could. "Do you?"

She exhaled. "Rowan, I do not—" Evie licked her lips and tried again. "I am confused by all of this and heartsore from all the events of the last few months. I don't know what this means or how it works. It seems unfair to Caelan."

The mention of his name felt like a knife sliding through my ribs. "Bonds do not care who came before." I touched her chin. "I know you're confused and working through things. If I would have known this bond would advance so much when claiming my land, I would not have allowed you to do so. Your power and mine are complementary, and we are both linked to the earth. It's the only explanation I have."

Her eyes searched mine. "And if I don't want this?"

It took everything I had to keep my face neutral, but my heart screamed in agony. "Then you can refuse this. You will have to leave and remove your claim on my lands and the other territory or remove me if you wish to keep your mark there. And then you must stay away. Eventually, the bond will fade."

"Our friendship would be over."

I nodded. "Every time we saw each other, the bonds would begin to reform. We could not see each other anymore. And it would be cruel to me to try."

Evie's lower lip wobbled. She lifted her hand and stroked my cheek. "I cannot give you an answer now, Rowan. As much as I wish I could do this, I am not ready for something so soon after Caelan."

She's right. We both know it, so all I could do was nod. I pressed a searing kiss to her lips and stepped away. "I'll send the staff in later with lunch. I think it's best if we do not go into town this morning. Not everyone will be able to see the bond between us, but some shifters have better senses than others."

"Will the other Lords sense the bond?"

She meant Caelan but didn't want to hurt my feelings. I inclined my head. "Yes. He will know."

Evie flinched, and my heart broke a little more. "But he will know the bond is not finished?"

"How close are we?"

I smiled. "Too close," was all the answer I could give her. I laid a hand over my chest. "Thank you for all you've done for me. No matter what happens, I will hold you forever close in my heart."

"Rowan." Her voice broke. She stepped forward, her hand outstretched, but I couldn't bear her touch.

I turned and walked away.

I left not long after Rowan walked away, cloaked in grief and the remnants of magic I'd expended on his land. Dad brought Moira to my house instead of Rowan's and said nothing, even though his eyes widened when he saw me.

Dad saw the bond as well. Moira and I sat on the couch, our feet touching as we sipped spiked hot chocolate.

"Damn," she said a few moments after I finished telling her everything that had happened.

"Yeah," I said with a sigh.

"Heavy stuff."

"Simone and Garrett are extremely pissed at you, FYI."

I groaned. "Totally forgot to tell them I was leaving."

"You're not used to having an entourage, but yes, you left them without a word, and now they have to take a flight home."

I winced. "I may need to give them a bonus."

"Or emotional hazard pay." Moira grinned to soften her words. "You know," she said thoughtfully, "I'm less surprised by this than I expected."

My eyebrows rose. "Oh?"

She lifted a slender shoulder in a shrug. "You've always gotten along with him to the point where Caelan was extremely jealous.

You let him through your wards and into your home, and you even let him hold you. I've never seen you do that with anyone else before. Not once."

"I trust him."

"And you let him share your territory when all of the other Lords would have showered you with gifts and titles and wifed you up to gain all those lands."

"I would have gifted it to him," I muttered under my breath. "He asked to share instead."

Moira snorted. "Sounds exactly like something that sweet, loving bastard would do, doesn't it?"

Her words made me belly laugh.

"You chose him. Not Caelan. Not Ben. Rowan. You gifted him the power of two Lords and didn't bat an eye. He allowed you to claim all of his lands even knowing how dangerous that might be to his standing. He's been in love with you for a while."

I jerked my attention to her. "What?"

"A blind man could see it." She sipped her cocoa. "Probably why Caelan gets so growly when Rowan is around. There's always been a thread of something between you. Close proximity sent that thread into hyperdrive."

"This is bad," I murmured.

"Is it?" Moira asked. "Or are you worried about what Caelan will think when he sees you?"

I closed my eyes, resisting the urge to scream. "I am not sure how I feel. There's something between us, but this is all too soon. I —I'm not ready."

She watched me over the top of her mug. "Who said you have to be?"

My brow furrowed.

"Is Rowan pushing you to accept?

"No." The opposite.

"Did he say it had to be now or never?"

I shook my head.

"Has he ever pushed you into accepting anything you didn't want?"

I blew out an annoyed breath and laughed. "I know what you're doing."

Moira gave me an innocent look. "Me?"

"You've always liked him."

"He makes it very difficult not to like him."

"Unlike Soren," I said, needling her a little bit.

"Soren can fall in a wolf-sized hole for all I care."

I blinked at the vehemence in her words. "Well," I said softly. "There's obviously a story there."

"A horror novel," Moira grumbled. She flicked her fingers at me. "But we aren't talking about me. We're talking of wonderful Rowan."

I grabbed the bottle of brandy and poured more in my cup, offering Moira some when I'd finished. She happily accepted. "Want my advice?" she asked.

"I'm not sure anymore."

Moira laughed. "Take care of your affairs here. Have it out with Caelan. Get the closure you need. Then decide. Either way, I'm not sure you'll be able to stay here if you break things off forever with him."

"I don't know where it all went so wrong."

Moira sighed and nudged my thigh with her toe. "He hunted you like a predator thinking you were prey. And when you proved anything but, the thrill of a challenge ignited his blood. But when you became too powerful for even him to handle, the dynamics between you changed and it turned him bitter."

I stared at my friend, dumbstruck. She smiled and clinked our cups together. "My dear, this was never about the children. This has always been about you and the threat you pose to his way of life. He's making excuses to justify his own shortcomings."

Could it be that easy? Had this always been about Caelan's need for control? I sat there and stared at Moira until she snorted.

"For someone so smart, sometimes you can be so dumb. Especially when it comes to matters of the heart."

"I've been a fool."

Moira clicked her tongue. "No. You've been a woman pursued by a handsome, powerful, sexy male who made you feel cherished and beautiful. Caelan would have always been happy in that position, content to have you by his side until you went and changed the game on him. He's not a man good with surprises. Or with women who outrank him." She sighed and snuggled deeper into the cushions. "It's a tale as old as time."

"Fuck," I muttered. "I have a lot to think about."

"Mmm hmm. You do. We should call Tess and Ash while we're here. They've been hearing rumblings around town about the swans and other things."

I closed my eyes and swore. "The swans. Shit." The swan shifters had come in hot and heavy with plans to kidnap me and forcibly impregnate me with swan babies to alleviate their infertility curse. Looking at things on the surface made their plan seem laughable, but they'd managed to take one of our people and we still hadn't found him. We'd killed one of their own and raided their Keep, but we all knew they weren't done with me yet. It was only a matter of when they might strike next. Not if.

Moira laughed. "The arrows are flying in all directions now."

"I'm thinking about killing all of them."

Surprise flashed in Moira's eyes. "Swift and decisive. I like it."

I loved her for never judging me no matter what harebrained shit I came up with.

"Not too bloodthirsty?"

"Those bastards want you for your womb and still have one of your people captive. You're well within your rights to finish wiping them off the map." A deadly grin tipped her lips up. "I'm happy to help."

"A better person would help them conceive."

"You and I have never been better people. We're survivors

living in a fucked-up world. The swans chose the path they're on. Let them see what lies at the end."

"I fucking love you, you bloodthirsty savage."

Moira winked. "I'm glad to see you getting back to normal."

"Let's give Ash and Tess a call. After that, I'm paying Caelan a visit."

"Oooh. Want us to come?"

I shook my head. "I'll be fine. If Caelan is on the fence about my power, I'm thinking I should give him the full show to help him decide."

We grinned at each other, and there was nothing soft in either one of our smiles.

I COULD HAVE KNOCKED, but I felt like sending a message more. After a call to my father who showed up immediately, we stood outside Caelan's slightly tweaked wards.

"You sure about this?" he asked. There's no judgment in his voice, but I don't miss the sparkle in his eyes. He's loving every second of this.

"You think I should be more diplomatic?"

Dad snorted. "Diplomacy is for people who lack power."

I laughed. "That's the response of a tyrant."

"No. It's the response of a man who knows he can pass right through these wards and stab your Lord right in the heart before he has a chance to move. It's the response of someone who can snap his fingers and crumble this Keep to dust. We are power made flesh, Evangeline, and if we can't use it to save ourselves and the people we love, what good are our gifts?"

"I loved him. I might still love him."

"Love comes in many different forms, daughter."

"So neutral, Dad. We both know you don't like Caelan."

"He, like all of the Lords, serves a purpose."

"Do you think I should leave this alone?"

Dad spears me with a look. "Caelan will never leave you alone if you do not excise him from your life. I will take care of what needs to be taken care of away from the Keep. Once you do this, things will quickly escalate."

"I wish things were different."

"You cannot change a mountain."

His face is calm and stoic, but anticipation glittered in his eyes. "He's not a mountain, Dad. He's a wolf. I've seen him try to be better."

Dad's eyes swirled. He cloaked us in invisibility as we stood outside, a shimmer of clear power keeping us hidden from the sight and enhanced senses of the other shifters. "I like it when you call me Dad. It's such a quaint, human word, more pleasurable to the ear than Father."

"Okay, weirdo."

We grinned at each other. "It has been a pleasure getting to know you, Evangeline. I know my apology may not be worth much, but I regret every day I was not in your life."

My eyes burned. "I wondered about you every single day. What you looked like. What foods you liked. If you would like me. For my entire life, I thought you were human."

Dad grimaced. "Very sorry to disappoint."

"I can't say I'm pleased with the whole crown thing, but over-all, I'm not too unhappy with how things turned out."

His side-eye was epic. "You definitely inherited your mother's mouth."

"As long as I don't inherit those creepy antlers."

Dad barked a laugh. "Those creepy antlers are part of your great heritage, daughter."

"They won't match anything in my closet." I nudged him and stepped forward.

"Once you do this, there is no going back, Evangeline."

"Are you urging me to be cautious?"

"Me?" Dad laughed. "If you'd seen me in my youth, my dear, you'd know I used caution like the most precious spice. A little here, a little there, never too much."

"And now?"

Dad grinned, a flash of white teeth in the night. "And now I find I tire of spice."

We were more like each other than not, and I wasn't sure how I felt about that. "You'd burn it all to the ground if you could."

"I still could. But I won't. It's bad for business."

"I'm not a businessman."

"Exactly. The Lord owes you a pound of flesh. Go take it."

With a snap of his fingers, the wind shifted direction, blowing my scent away from the Keep and out into the forest. If Caelan came close enough, he might scent the bond on me. Tonight would be difficult enough. If I could keep this secret until I figured out what to do, I could save Caelan from more heartache.

Not that he deserved much from me after everything, but I would always care about him. Even if he didn't care about me, not in the way I deserved.

Concentrating magic in my hands, I focused power in one spot just like my father had shown me and slammed my hand against his wards.

"Good luck," Dad said as he faded away.

Power clanged like a bell inside my head. Gritting my teeth, I pushed magic into the wards. They flashed with lightning forks of crimson, painting the Keep with the color of blood. He'd tweaked them again since I'd left, though I could have flown in if I were in wren form. Not today. I wanted to make a statement.

A loud crack rang out as the wards crashed and fell, allowing me to step onto Caelan's lands without harm.

Shouts rang out as shifters flooded from the doors of the main area of the Keep. They saw me and stumbled, surprise flashing over their faces as I stood in the middle of the property.

Caelan walked out behind them.

"I wondered when you'd show up."

My heart dropped into my feet, but that tug, the yearning to go to him was no longer there. I loved him, that had always been true, but a gulf stood between us now, a yawning chasm too deep for me to cross. All my hopes and dreams lay shattered at the bottom, promises made and cast aside, tender words and secret touches, all broken and torn.

Caelan was beautiful, had always been beautiful. He probably always would be. Tall and handsome, and those familiar storm-colored eyes, I remembered the feel of his hands gliding over my skin, how much I wanted him, how much he made me feel.

All I felt now was grief.

I spread my arms out and smiled. "Here I am."

He stopped several feet away. A tall man I'd never seen before stepped up beside him. "You're dismissed," Caelan said.

"Lord." The man looked at me with fear. I was the wolf in the garden when Caelan only saw a rabbit.

"She is my fiancée," Caelan said. "We'll be in shortly."

We wouldn't. I smiled at the man I assumed to be his new Second.

He blinked and took a step back. "Lord."

"Leave us," Caelan snapped.

The shifter gave me a long look before he turned, motioning to the others to follow.

When everyone was back inside, Caelan came closer, but not close enough to scent Rowan's lands on my skin. As soon as tomorrow, the Lords might know what I'd done, how I'd given more power to one Lord than a single man has ever had. Dario would have felt me removing his mark on my lands. Our lands now, I supposed.

"Such a dramatic entrance for a homecoming. Was there really a need to tear down my wards?"

"No. I wanted you to know how powerless you are against me."

Caelan blinked and burst out laughing a second later. "Are you trying to strike fear into my heart, Evie? I'd think such was beneath you."

"What happened to us?" The question was out of my mouth before I could stop the words. I'd come here to prove a point but seeing him standing in front of me was breaking my heart. "All those promises we made to each other. How hard we fought to be together. How did it all fall apart?"

For the first time in months, Caelan was speechless.

"We loved each other so much, and now when I look at you, I see a stranger." I can't stop myself from pouring my heart out. "You are not the man I swore my life to, and I'm not sure what happened to break us."

Caelan's face went blank, but his eyes burned. "I began with a Floromancer who possessed a spine of steel and ended with a cursed queen."

His words stab through the broken shell of my heart. "I am the same woman I always was."

His laugh cuts me. "You are no woman at all."

"Caelan." I no longer know who he is. "You evicted us from my shop unless I returned to you and you still say these things to me."

"Are you returning to me? Even after all this, I still want you and being king would have its perks," he mused. "But the way you look at me, Evie." He tsked. "You are not here to stand by my side, are you? And if you are, you plan to slip a knife between my ribs when I'm sleeping."

"Do you want me to fall on my knees, Lord? Profess my undying love to you?"

Caelan laughed, the sound like ice in my heart. There's no warmth to the tone. He knows I'm mocking him. "A Lady knows her place. Even when you were the Chimera, you deferred to my judgment, but when your true heritage was revealed, you weakened my position with my shifters."

I stared at him. "All this because I outranked you?" My fury makes the ground tremble. "If we were married, all of those problems would be gone."

"The heir issue would still exist. I chose you when you were a Floromancer, stayed and reveled in your power when you revealed your true nature, but when you became the queen, you weakened my rule."

He came a few steps closer and the light caught on his cheek revealing a small black smudge. My breath caught, the hurt from his words replaced with alarm. "Caelan. What is that on your cheek?"

He touched his cheek. "None of your concern. The Keep Healers are treating me."

"Have you felt different lately? Is your power stable?"

"Why so curious about me now, Evie? You came here to end things for good."

It was a struggle to keep my temper in check. "There is a powerful spell corrupting this country's land. I cleansed Rowan's territory, but I had to claim a portion to keep the magic at bay." He didn't need to know I'd claimed all of it with Rowan's blessing. "If you allow me, I'll cleanse your lands as well and heal the spot on your cheek."

His brows drew together. "Why would you do this for me?"

My smile was full of heartbreak. "Because I loved you more than myself once."

His answering smile almost broke my resolve. "My people have to come first, Evie."

"You could have had everything if you just waited a little while longer. I would have protected your people, given my life for them and for you."

His irises ringed with gold. "It's not your job to protect them, and I cannot ally with the fae against my people and the other Lords."

I wanted to strangle him. "Is that what you saw our union as? A betrayal to your own?" A harsh laugh cracked from my throat. "If you would have only trusted me, things could have been so different."

"Loyalty is soul deep, Evangeline. My blood belongs to this land, to the shifters behind me."

"I deserved your loyalty!" The scream shattered the night. "I would have given you everything, and you pushed me away like I was last night's leftovers."

"After time, I realized there would be no mating bond."

"You said yourself that successful marriages and partnerships exist without one."

"I am a Lord. My people deserve a true mating bond."

"So all that pomp and circumstance after my shift to the Chimera was bullshit?"

His jaw tightened. Caelan had claimed me as his Lady but never made it true. His people had never accepted me. To make it worse, he never again made the declaration the same way, making me feel like he'd forgotten about me or went back on his word. Most of his people had been wary of me and stayed that way the entire time we were together.

Not like—

I cut the thought of Rowan off.

"Things are different now." Caelan made no move to come closer, stared at me like we were strangers. Maybe we were.

"Yes," I agreed. "They are." Shaking my head, I tried to reorder my thoughts. "We have to stop going in circles. This is our death knell. I'll be out of your territory within the allotted time, but I refuse to give up my property until I'm good and ready. I'm the owner, not you. Until then, my offer stands. Allow me to temporarily claim the borders of your territory until this dark magic is brought under control. I'll heal you as well."

Caelan's eyes glowed. "Is this the fae plan to seize territory back from the Lords?"

My temper snapped. "Oh, for fuck's sake, Caelan. Stop being a sniveling brat and listen to me. I've never lied to you. You've been feeling poorly. Parts of your land are dying. That mark on your cheek is the first manifestation of it consuming you. Allow me to help you. Do not let your pride stand in the way of my assistance."

For a moment, he wavered, and I thought we'd reach some

sort of truce. But once again, pride won over reason. Caelan's jaw tightened, and claws slid from his fingertips.

"Get off my lands." Gone was the Lord I knew, the male I loved. In its place stood a prideful, stubborn-beyond-all-reason Lord. One who wanted to protect his people at the cost of his own happiness.

I tried one more time. "Caelan, please. Don't do this. Let me help you."

He scoffed. "Help me? You've ruined everything."

"I will not let you die because you refuse to see reason."

"Get. Off. My. Lands." His arms grew fur, his canines sliding into wicked fangs.

Shifters exited the main door, coming to stand a few feet away until I was surrounded. "I'm sorry it's come to this," I said softly.

I reached for my power and *yanked*. A circular barrier shot up from the ground, enclosing us in a cage of green. Caelan snarled. The sounds of shifters howling and tearing through the natural barricade sent a shiver down my spine. But I wouldn't leave until I gave Caelan a chance.

"Will you take my lands by force, Evie?" The words were garbled by his fangs.

"No, you idiot. But I will do this." Vines shot from the ground and wrapped around him, trapping his hands against his sides, flowing all the way to his jawline, keeping the Lord immobile. I lunged toward him, magic at the ready, and slapped my hand against his damaged cheek. Dark magic screamed against my skin. Watermelon tourmaline-colored power poured from my palms soaking his face with light. I concentrated, sweeping through his body to destroy every inch of the spell affecting him, not stopping until I found no trace of any more darkness.

I stepped back and studied him. Caelan stared at me like he'd seen a ghost. His hand crept up and touched his cheek.

"Feel better?" I didn't add asshole to the end, but he deserved it.

His eyes narrowed. "I won't thank you."

"Surprise, surprise," I said with a click of my tongue. "I've only bought you time today. If you won't accept my help, that spell will continue to run unhindered through your lands. Eventually, it will infect you again. This is my final offer. Accept my assistance, or I will not return to help you again."

A muscle in his cheek twitched. "Leave," he said after a long pause.

I slipped the ring off my finger and dropped it in the dirt. "Despite everything, I only want the best for you, even if it's not with me. I would have loved you for the rest of my days, Caelan."

Without giving him a chance to respond, I shifted into my fae form and rose above the barrier. With a thought, I released Caelan from the vines and allowed the barricade to fall.

Then I turned my back and flew away, stopping only when I was safely out of reach from his people. From there, I shifted and called Dad.

"Everything ready?"

"Yes. Moira, Tess, and Ash are with me. They have news."

"I'm ready."

Dad said nothing for a beat. "It went that well?"

I snorted so I wouldn't cry. "Can you show me how to keep Caelan and his people from my lands while I figure out what to do?"

"I'll show you later. For now, I'll ensure they remain safe."

"Thank you. I'll meet you at the place we discussed."

"I'm sorry things went south."

Me too. "I planned for things to end the way they did. See you all in a bit."

We disconnected. I pulled out one of Moira's precious travel potions and downed it, concentrating on the place I wanted to go.

CHAPTER
Twenty-Seven
CAELAN

An emergency meeting notice went out later that evening from the wannabe new Lord, Dario. I thought about ignoring it, but the second text that came in gave me serious pause.

Rowan's mark was on Donovan's old land, somehow merged with Evie's magic.

She'd given him a claim to territory that belonged to the Lords.

Rage bloomed in my veins. Evie had stolen everything from me. My good name, my Omega and Second, Seymour and Hannah, my heart, and now land that rightfully belonged to us. But not only had she taken the land, she'd shared it with someone who was not me.

I picked up the phone.

He answered on the first ring. "I've been expecting a call from you."

"Why?" was all I could say.

"She trusts me. I did not ask. Evie offered."

"You didn't think this was a decision for the Council?"

Rowan snorted. "So you could fight like dogs over a bone and squabble over petty politics rather than act as a true steward of the land?"

Disgust filled me. "Cut this shit," I snarled. "You took the land to secure more power for yourself."

Rowan's laugh sent my hackles up. "You think in terms of what you would do. All these years and you still don't realize I don't give a shit about power. I stay within the boundaries of my territory, rarely engage unless directly threatened, and try my best to keep the peace within the Council. I am not like you. I never have been. Evie can take that land back any time she wants to, and I wouldn't bat an eye. She saw Dario trying to claim the land from under her nose and booted him out. That right there shows how fairly the Lords play. He hasn't been officially approved by the Council yet and he's already staking a claim."

"That's Donovan's land."

"Evie won the land by might and right. If you want to get deep in the woods about things, none of the land we hold belongs to us. We're here by the grace of the fae. This land belongs to them and always has. They don't want to be involved in petty human politics and allow us to govern."

My laugh is mirthless. "I knew this was a way for the fae to reclaim their position."

"She visited you, didn't she?"

"What of it?"

He let out a heavy sigh. "You refused her help. Of course you did. You fool."

"Evie has taken all she will ever get from me."

"You will die if you do not allow her to help."

I touched my cheek and wondered how true his words were. "I'll take my chances."

Rowan changed the subject. "She would have stayed with you forever, Caelan."

I didn't want to think about what my life would have been like if I'd stayed with her. I made the right choice, didn't I? "Evie could not have given me what I needed."

The other Lord sighed. "Love? Power? Meaning? She could

have given you all of that and more, but you were a stubborn fool and chose to cast her out."

"My people come first!" I heard the words and realized they sounded hollow.

"Your people would have been protected for the rest of their lives with her standing as their Lady."

"She could not give me heirs."

Rowan's anger crackled over the line. "Heirs that you approved of. How very elitist of you, Lord."

The word dripped with condescension.

"You can have her." My words are petulant and sound childish.

Rowan laughed. "I will be lucky if she comes back to me after what you've done to her. You will reap what you've sowed, Caelan. Mark my words."

"Enjoy my used seconds."

I'd gone too far. Even over the telephone, I could feel his rage. And when he spoke once more, I knew I'd shattered our friendship into dust. "When we next meet, we will meet as enemies. Speak of my mate like that again, and I will revel in tearing the flesh from your bones."

The line went dead.

His mate.

Rowan and Evie were *mates.*

What had I done?

The phone crumbled into metal in my hands.

CHAPTER

Twenty~Eight

He met me on the grounds, about a half-mile away from his residence. Hands tucked into his pockets and an unreadable look on his handsome face, he watched me approach.

I stopped a few feet away, my heart pounding like a drum. "I seek refuge for me and my people."

My father, Moira, Tess, and Ash stood just off the edge of his wards waiting to see what would happen.

One of his dark eyebrows rose. "Your people?"

I nodded. "And, um, my shop."

His lips twitched. "Does this have anything to do with the phone call I just received from a very angry Lord in Texas?"

I cringed. "Would it help if I say he started it?"

"Did he start it?"

My shoulders slumped. "No. I shattered his wards."

Rowan let out a belly laugh.

The sound lightened my heavy heart. But I had to be honest with him. "I—I can't promise you anything. Not right now. I need time. What I can say is I feel this, too. There's something between us, something pure and good, but I can't move on this quickly. It's not fair to either one of us. Or Caelan."

He grimaced and shoved a hand through his hair. "I'm guilty of antagonizing him as well. Caelan knows what we are to each other."

I stared at him for a long moment. "I'll assume there's a reason you told him."

"Well, he pissed me off."

I rubbed a hand over my face and let out a sad little laugh. "Not the best reason, but I've done some things when I'm angry that haven't ended well for me."

"He said some unforgivable things. Unlike him, I do not allow others to speak ill of those I love."

I jogged over and wrapped my arms around him. Rowan lifted me up and I buried my face in the crook of his shoulder, inhaling his wild scent.

"You weren't gone long, but I missed you," he murmured against my skin. "I wasn't sure you'd be back."

"I knew I wouldn't stay there. Not after everything. If you'll have me, I'll find a place in town somewhere. But I might need help finding a place for Moira and the others. And I'll need to figure out the shop." A sigh escaped me. "This sucks."

"You and your people will stay on Keep property. Tomorrow, or whenever you're ready, I'll have Hope take you into town and search for a new place."

"About that." I pulled back. "Dad did some wizard stuff and took my entire shop."

Rowan stilled. "Like the brick and mortar and all of it?"

"Sort of, I think? Dad can explain it better than me. All I know is everything is sort of floating in space waiting for a new spot."

His grip tightened. "You do keep things interesting." Rowan tucked a strand of my hair behind my ear. "You don't have to make any decisions now. My offer has no strings attached."

I framed his face with my hands. "Are you sure? I don't want things to be weird between us. And I don't mind finding a rental or something until I can settle in."

His palm settled over my hand. "I am not Caelan. Nothing I offer you has strings. All I ask is that you tend the land." Rowan's soft smile soothes the jagged edges of my heart. "The place likes you, and you claimed it, so that will be the rent payment. Do we have a deal?"

I search his face for any cunning or manipulation and see only honesty shining from his hazel eyes. "What about Moira and the others?"

"We have community nights. Declan puts together a monthly schedule of duties, things like cooking, cleaning, etc. I can have him add the others."

"I'll ask, but they don't plan to stay too long. Just enough to find an apartment or house. They'll be happy to help while they're here, though."

"Hope will assist them, too."

"Thank you. You cannot understand how grateful I am to you for everything you've done for me. I hope I'm able to somehow repay you for your generosity."

He pressed a finger to my lips. "No strings, Evie. Never between us."

Rowan dropped his finger. I pressed forward and brushed my lips over his. He stilled, breath catching. My fingers scratched through his hair and deepened the kiss before I pulled away. He tasted like wind and rain and other deeper things I couldn't afford to think about. "A little time. That's all I ask."

His eyes burned molten gold. "You will have it." He set me down but kept his arm around my waist. "The others can come in now."

Dad and everyone else appeared a moment later, walking through the fog. Hope came from the opposite direction, waving when she spotted me.

"Simone and Garrett?" I asked.

"On their way back from the airport," Hope said with a wince. "They're pretty pissed at you."

"I'll figure out a way to make things up to them. Do they still have a place to stay?"

"No one cleaned out their quarters yet. Garrett has expressed interest in moving into town with Thalia."

I blinked. "Wow. Together?"

Hope laughed. "Yes, but I don't think their relationship has progressed as fast as he wants it to."

She motioned everyone over once they got close enough. "We have an empty apartment available for a few nights until we can arrange something for a longer period. It's a hike, so we'll run by the main house to get a golf cart."

Tess and Ash followed her, but not before they both drew me into a tight hug.

Moira came over and took my hands. "You okay?"

I gave her the brightest smile I could muster. "I will be."

She touched my cheek and stepped back. "You will." Moira turned her attention to Rowan. "Thank you for being what Evie needed."

He inclined his head and watched her walk away, his eyes still glowing. Dad, who stayed back, waved and disappeared in a flash of light.

When we were alone, Rowan held his hand out. "Your room is still open. Tomorrow, we can discuss what's next."

I walked with Rowan further onto the grounds of my new home.

THE NEXT MORNING everyone gathered around the large breakfast table in the main residence. Hope had a map spread out, dotted with blue and green push pins. "This is where you three stayed last night."

She pointed to one of the green pins. "This is where Evie was staying." Another green pin.

"We have a two-bedroom apartment here." She pointed to one of the blue pins. The place stands alone and away from the main dormitories. "A one bedroom here." The next pin is closer to the main house. "And there's a small two-bedroom home at the back of the main residence here, close to the greenhouse."

I peered closer at the map. "I never noticed this place."

"It's hidden by a bunch of trees and about a quarter mile away from here." She lifted her eyes. "Rowan and I think this is the best option for you. You'll be able to tend those new roses you brought while also having close access to the golf carts when you want to explore other areas of the property."

I felt a little numb today, still heartsick over yesterday's events. Today, everything was different. I was back with Rowan, and being back on his land made my spirit a little more settled than before. Knowing there's no possibility of returning to Joy Springs hurt my heart and made it difficult to be happy or feel relieved about anything. The home I'd made with my friends no longer existed for us. Maybe it would for Ash and Tess, possibly even Moira if they asked, but the life I'd had when the attack destroyed my old one was gone.

Sometimes you have to lose everything to gain something better.

"There's a kitchen and everything?" I asked her.

"Of course. It's small but serviceable and it lets in a lot of natural light so you can grow whatever plants you want inside."

Hope smiled at me, and I had trouble returning the gesture. I was truly grateful, but it would take a while for me to settle in and accept this new way of life. Her eyes softened and she rose from her hunch. "Declan will take you to the apartments." Rowan's second came in a second later, shaking a pair of keys in his hands. "You'll have to decide who shares and who lives alone."

Tess and Ash look at each other. "Moira can have the one bedroom."

The vampire's eyebrows flick up, but she doesn't argue. "Thanks again for having us. In a few days I'll start looking around town for a new place. If you have any leads on some houses with some land, I'm game to look at them."

Before they left, I reached out and tugged Moira's hand. "When Rowan gets back, I'll talk to him about setting the shop back up, but I don't expect anyone to start working right away. All of this is a massive shock." Tears filled my eyes. "I'm grateful and humbled you came with me, but if you ever want to go back, I will never stand in your way."

Moira snorted. "Like that will happen."

Tess and Ash came over and hugged me from behind. "We already told you home is wherever we're together." Ash ruffled my hair and brushed a kiss over my cheek. "If Rowan is okay with it, I may ask to have my tree moved to his lands. This place is incredible."

"I'll let him know you're looking for him."

Ash winked and followed Declan out, Moira and Tess behind them. Hope folded up her map and tucked into her bag. "Ready? It's not too far to walk if you're up for it."

"Fresh air would do me some good."

The morning air was cold and crisp. I tied my sweater closed and walked beside Hope. "I'm sorry to hear what happened," she began. "But I'm not sorry to see you back so soon and to know you'll be with us permanently. No matter what type of relationship you were in with him, breaking up is never easy."

She led us down a stone path past the greenhouse and a few smaller buildings. "I thought I knew him, and maybe I did, but I didn't understand his motivations or what drove him enough to realize he'd sacrifice me if I got in the way of realizing them."

Hope's mouth tightened. "Every shifter is different, just like humans, but wolves are a different breed. Caelan has long been known to be ruthlessly driven. None of us thought he'd go so far. Not even Rowan."

"They've been friends for many years, haven't they?"

Hope hesitated before admitting, "Yes. They were."

I stumble over a stone. Hope's hand reaches out to steady me. "Were?"

"Declan and I know what you are to each other."

At my look, she held up a hand. "Almost are, I should say. Rowan is fiercely protective of his people, but you…" Hope shook her head. "The bond might not be completed, but Rowan has always treated you like something precious. Now with the bond almost completed, he would never allow anyone to speak ill of you. Not even another Lord."

I'm terrified for him. Wherever I go, trouble seems to follow. "He doesn't need to protect me."

Hope and I turned a sharp corner hidden behind a copse of trees to reveal an adorable dark blue cottage. I sucked in a breath and stopped in my tracks. "This is the cutest thing I've ever seen."

The Omega laughed. "He had it built a year or so ago, but no guests have stayed inside."

I frowned. "Whyever not? I could be the perfect witch of the woods living in this thing."

Hope grinned and opened the maroon door. I ran my fingers over the wood and gasped in delight. "The paint is non-toxic."

Hope glanced at me in surprise and laughed. "I forget what you are sometimes. Yes. The entire house is all eco-friendly."

I walked inside and fell in love. The floors are gnarled and natural, sealed with Tung oil. "Oh my gosh." I dropped to my knees and ran my fingers over the floor. "Tung oil sealant?"

"Rowan had that done a few months ago." Hope watched me as her words finally registered.

I looked up. "Did he suspect I might be here one day?"

Hope shrugged. "More hope than anything."

Stunned, I sat down on the floor and let out a long breath, but I was having trouble breathing. My heart pounded in my chest, and my breath rasped in my lungs. Everything was overwhelming. My fingers shook and my entire body trembled.

Hope came to her knees beside me, one hand resting on my back. "Evie. Breathe. You're having a panic attack."

My vision pinpointed to a small circle, and stars bloomed behind my eyes.

"Put your head between your knees," she instructed.

When I obey, the first tears leak from my eyes. Hope rubbed small circles over my shoulders. A sob escaped me, and once it started, I couldn't seem to stop. Tears dripped on the floor, and hoarse, devastated noises ripped from my throat.

"Oh Evie," Hope whispered. She gathered me in her arms, and a torrent of grief poured from me, my broken heart finally safe enough to break. I hate that it's with Hope, and I hate that she's seeing me in one of my most vulnerable moments, but grief never works on a timeline.

I had no idea how long I sat there, sobbing my heart out, but eventually the body holding me changed. Strong arms lifted me from the floor and cradled me against a muscled chest, a deep voice murmuring words of comfort against my hair.

I clutched Rowan's shirt and buried my face in his chest. And still, the tears kept coming. My voice grew hoarse, and yet I still can't stop. My body had finally stopped listening to my commands and started purging the poison I'd been holding in for so long.

Rowan's hand stroked through my hair, his lips pressed against my temple, and he pulled me closer into his body as he sat down on the couch. "Get it out," he whispered to me. "You've been so strong for so long, Evie. You don't have to be anymore. You're safe. I have you. There's no one else but you and me here, and we don't have anywhere else to be."

I couldn't even respond. My eyes burned, my throat dry. All my self-recrimination and doubt poured out in the form of hot tears, and no matter how much I wanted them to stop, they wouldn't. After some time, Rowan re-adjusted us until we were lying down, and I curled against his body, arms wrapped tight around me.

My heartbeat finally began to slow, and my sobs turned into soft hiccups. My tears dried up, and exhaustion, both physical and emotional, seeped into my bones. But the poison was purged, and though my life hasn't turned out quite like I thought it would, it hasn't turned out bad.

I was here with a man who seemed to cherish me, and I felt safe, truly safe being vulnerable for one of the very few times in my life. My eyes slowly drifted shut, and sleep claimed me moments later.

CHAPTER

Twenty~Nine

I awoke covered in flowers and vines. Blinking the sleep from my eyes, I frowned as an unfamiliar ceiling loomed above me. It took me a minute to remember where I was.

"Rowan?" I croaked.

My cheeks turned crimson as I remembered what happened. The Lord poked his head out from around the corner and sent a critical eye from my face all the way down to my toes.

"Hi," I said. My voice was hoarse from overuse.

His eyes crinkled at the edges. "Hey. I made some lunch if you're hungry."

I sat up and brushed away the flowers, frowning at them. I hoped this wasn't a new thing to happen every time I went to sleep. The vines fell away as I swung my legs over the side of the couch. With a whispered command, the greenery disappeared.

My stomach growled, making Rowan laugh. "Don't get up. I'll bring you a bowl."

I tugged a blanket across my lap and waited, inhaling the scent of something delicious. Rowan came in holding a tray with two bowls of something steaming, fresh-cut bread and a saucer of golden butter. Moira followed him in holding a pot of coffee and several mugs. Ash came behind her holding a pitcher of something cold, and Tess walked behind him holding a few glasses.

I blinked at the sight of them, and I felt my face crumple once again. But this time, I wasn't crippled by heartbreak. All I felt was happiness they'd chosen to follow me. I could do many things, but living without them wasn't a life I wanted to live.

Moira sat beside me, so close our thighs touched, and poured me a mug of coffee. I curled my hands around the mug and gave her a wobbly smile. Moira responded by laying her head on my shoulder for a moment.

"I love you, Evie."

"Love you back."

Ash and Tess settled into chairs next to each other. Rowan set the tray down and sat on my other side.

"Are you guys hungry?" I asked, noting there were only two bowls.

Everyone shook their heads. "Declan fed us before we came over," Ash said.

"The apartments are wonderful," Tess added, a sparkle in her pale eyes. "These lands are perfect for a banshee to haunt."

Rowan blinked at that one.

"I can sense a few banshees somewhere within the boundaries. Maybe I'll try to find them later."

Rowan opened his mouth and shut it before saying anything. His nonplussed expression made me chuckle. "You get used to it," I said quietly. "Tess is one in a million."

"I have banshees?" Rowan asked. His expression is bemused.

Tess nodded enthusiastically. "At least two. You're lucky," she added. "If you haven't heard their screams, your people all have healthy lifespans ahead of them." Tess smiled. "So far."

With that ominous note, Rowan shook his head and let out a little laugh. "Alright. We'll leave them be and hope not to hear any screaming."

Tess blessed Rowan with a beaming smile. Ash chuckled under his breath and poured himself a glass of tea.

"Here," Rowan said, passing me a bowl sitting on a saucer. "I don't often cook because of my schedule, but I make a mean potato soup. The bread is courtesy of our local pastry chef."

"Thank you." Our eyes met, and I saw no judgment or disgust. Only a warm concern and something more.

He handed me a spoon. "Eat up. There's plenty more in the kitchen."

Soon enough, I'd focused on my soup, and everyone else was chatting about their plans to settle into their new places. As I sat there, seeing how animated my friends were and how easily they were adapting to this massive change, something in my heart eased, and for the first time, I relaxed.

Not too long after, everyone made their excuses and left, but not without a tight hug from each of them. When Rowan and I were the only ones left, he shifted his body to watch me closer. "Are you alright?"

My cheeks heated. "I'm okay. I think I needed a good cry. I'm sorry I—"

Rowan's eyes flashed with anger. "Never apologize for being vulnerable. Grief and anger are poison if left untended." His face softened. "Yours were long left untended. I do not know everything you've been through, but I know that was more than Caelan. I hope this is the first step toward a new beginning."

My lower lip wobbled. "I don't know how to not be careful anymore. I've kept everything bottled up for so long it feels natural to keep secrets now. I had to in order to keep myself and everyone I loved safe."

"Everyone has secrets, but the weight gets easier to carry when you share the burden."

He sat his mug down and opened his arms. "Come. I quite like the feeling of you against me."

I laughed at the earnest words.

Rowan gave me a roguish grin and wiggled his eyebrows. I scoot over and settle in between his legs, my back pressed against his chest. His contented sigh made me blush. My chest warmed in the spot of our bond, a soft and gentle heat. I could almost feel him there right at the edge of my senses.

"There's no other furniture in the house. If you decide to stay here, you can pick out whatever you want."

"I have plenty of money. Moira and the others should be financially secure for a while."

"Your shop is closed and business has been down for months now."

I tensed in his arms.

"Simone told me," Rowan said. "Caelan has not been good to you, despite how you might feel."

He's not wrong, but it chafes to realize how I've allowed myself to be treated. "The business took a hit," I admit, "but we're all good savers, and my father gave me access to a bank account. He calls it my inheritance."

"Odd word for a man who will never die."

"True. I'll need to order the furniture unless there's a place around here with sustainable practices."

"I forget how sensitive you are to certain things. Is this couch okay?"

"I don't have any bare skin touching the surface. Bedroom furniture is the most important. All my furniture back in Joy Springs would—" I stopped and groaned. "I can just call Dad to move it."

"Handy power, that," Rowan mused. "There's a spot in the middle of downtown that's for sale. I don't know how large your shop was in the back, but it might work. We can go tomorrow if you want."

"Starting over might be nice," I mused. "That sounds good." I sighed and closed my eyes. "Caelan was sick when I found him."

Rowan tensed behind me. "The spell?"

I nodded. "He refused my help, but I forced a healing on him to buy the idiot more time. I don't know how far the spell has reached within his borders. I need to speak to the other Lords soon."

"They're meeting tomorrow," Rowan said, his voice close to a growl. "Ethan called an emergency meeting."

"They know what we did." Unsurprising. I'd been waiting for that for a while now.

"They do, and they're less than enthused about things."

I chuckled. "Can they do anything about it?"

"Dario can challenge me for it."

I jerked upright and turned to face him. "That's our land. Not Dario's."

His eyes are soft when he reaches up to brush my cheek with his fingers. "Ours," he said quietly. "I like that word coming from your lips."

I stared at him and wondered what would have happened had I chosen him first. Too heartsore to move forward as fast as I wanted, I could only hope I won't hurt him in the future. Possibility reached between us, unfurling with potential. "He'd be an idiot to challenge you," I grumbled.

"He's young and arrogant. Regardless, I'd like you to come with me. We can appeal to the Lords' sensibilities and hope they see reason."

"What if Dario challenges you?" I'd never seen Rowan in a true fight. He charmed his way out of most conflicts, unlike the other testosterone-laden Lords. None of them were slouches in the physical prowess department or they wouldn't hold or maintain so much power. If Dario pushed things, I had no doubt Rowan could easily take him down.

"It's our land, as you said. He'll have to challenge us both, and I'm not sure he will."

The thought intrigued me. "It's been a while since I've kicked someone's ass."

Rowan snorted. "There's the feisty Evie I know."

"Caelan will be there tomorrow."

Rowan inhaled. "He will. I understand if you don't want to go. Being with me will send a statement. If you aren't ready, I'm happy to attend without you."

"I'm not worried about being seen with you."

The tension in his form relaxes. "I'm happy to hear that."

"Caelan may not react well. I don't want to make any problems for you."

He nuzzled my ear. "I'm well equipped to handle Caelan." His warm breath against my ear sent a shiver down my spine. My neck arched, and I froze, embarrassment heating my skin.

"Oh," Rowan breathed. "Your ear is sensitive. Duly noted." His teeth gently clamp onto the lobe, the flick of his tongue dragging a low moan from my throat.

I had no idea such a small touch could draw such a visceral response. Every nerve ending was on fire. That spot in my chest heated, a flicker of warmth floating between us, and I felt Rowan's desire, how much he wanted me.

Rowan tilted my neck and pressed a kiss below my ear. The urge to turn around and throw myself at him is almost overwhelming. His hands stayed locked at my waist, but his lips kept busy, teasing and tasting until I was a quivering mess of need.

"Rowan," I whispered.

"Hmm."

"We have to stop."

"You aren't doing anything."

A breathless laugh escaped me.

"Just stay right here, and I'll let you know when I'm finished." He smiled against my neck.

I tilted my head back and peered up at him. Rowan looked more relaxed than I'd ever seen him. His eyes looked green in the low light, and his hair and clothes were rumpled. "I'll stand by your side tomorrow," I said quietly. "I'll always stand by your side. I don't know where things will take us, but you will always have an ally in me."

"You can stay here as long as you want. I want you to stay at the Keep. Having you here makes everyone happy."

I grinned up at him. "Your shifters are a bunch of hippies."

Rowan snorted.

"Flower loving hippies."

"My people have always been more sensitive to the earth's call. Ever since you claimed the land with me, there hasn't been a single fight break out in the dorms." He grinned. "And I expect there to be a baby boom here in about nine months."

I blinked in surprise. "Seriously?"

Rowan nodded. "Yes. Lots of noise complaints came in that same night."

A giggle escaped me. "That's a little embarrassing."

"Are you kidding? I kept getting calls from the local police all night about the howling disrupting the populace. The entire Keep was blasting Barry Manilow. Total madness."

My eyes narrowed. "You're shitting me."

He held a hand up. "I swear. Whatever you did got their engines running."

I cackled. "Should I apologize?"

"Not even a little. Half the wolves wanted to go to Joy Springs and bring you back by force."

"Huh. I never thought about the ramifications of doing what I did when all the shifters were still on the land. Did you have any ill effects?"

A slow, sexy grin spread over his face. "I'm still holding those ill effects in if you're interested."

I snorted and tried to sit up. He groaned as he loosened his grip. "Spoilsport."

I stood and leaned over him, cupping his cheek in my hand. "You are wonderful, and I care about you very much, but I am not ready for anything physical."

He watched me, his hazel eyes serious. "I know. Nibbling on your ear is a great distraction from everything else going on, isn't it?"

I gasped in mock outrage. "I know that must have been very difficult for you. My neck must taste terrible, and I know I smell like a troll. You've been quite the trooper."

Rowan's eyes glinted with a dangerous light. "I do sacrifice for the people I care about."

"I can assure you your job is done. You'll never have to undergo such a trial ever again."

Rowan reached out and jerked me forward. I squawked and pinwheeled right into his arms. He nuzzled my neck. "You smell like heaven and taste like ambrosia."

"Flatterer."

Rowan chuckled. "Come on. Let's go back to the house and get some dinner. You can call your dad and see if he can transport all your furniture over."

He rose and lifted me with him, gently setting me on my feet. "Feeling better?"

I felt like a heavy weight had lifted from my shoulders, one I had carried for years and years. My breath came easier, my muscles were more relaxed. My heart still ached, but it was no longer the stabbing, tearing pain I experienced when I thought of Caelan. I leaned my head against his shoulder. "I am. Thank you."

He slung an arm over my shoulders. "No need to thank me. Touch-starved, remember? Anytime you want to snuggle, I'm your guy."

"Do you ever shift and get into a bear puppy pile with the other shifters?"

He gave me an odd look. "Why? Would you want to join?"

I tilted my head in thought. "I dunno. Maybe. I bet it'd be warm."

"Everyone is naked when they wake up, FYI." His eyes sparkled with amusement.

"You saw what happened when we got trapped in the cage."

Rowan closed his eyes. "Mmm. I sure did."

I punched him in the shoulder. "What are you feeding me tonight?"

"Whatever the chef is cooking."

"Spoken like a true Lord."

D ad came through. The next morning, the small cottage was filled with my most important things. All my clothing was in the master closet, and my toiletries were deposited in the bathroom closet. He'd brought my bedroom furniture and all my pots and pans and spices.

Most importantly, he'd brought all my shelves and plants.

"Holy shit," Rowan said when he stepped into the room. "Looks like a jungle in here."

"I need to organize everything." Hope was right about all the natural light coming through the windows. Even in an area of gray days, the house was brighter than my other had ever been. "The living room window is amazing. Most of the plants will thrive there."

Rowan was dressed in a pair of dark gray slacks, shiny black shoes, a dark blue pullover sweater that brought out the green flecks in his eyes. His hair was artfully mussed and he'd shaved this morning. My fingers itched to trace the line of his jaw.

"Evie?" His tone held a wealth of amusement.

I picked up a snake plant and carried it to the window. "Hmm?"

"You're still in your pajamas."

I took two of the pothos and arranged them on the small shelf Dad brought from the house. "Maybe too much light." I clicked my tongue.

"Evie?"

"Hmm?"

"Did you forget what we have to do today?"

I set down the pothos and turned to him with a frown. Realization dawned a second later. "Shit. Shit!" I clapped my hand over my mouth. Today was the emergency meeting with the Lords. "What should I wear?"

"Whatever you want to."

Yanking on his hand, I dragged him to my bedroom and started flinging clothes aside. "You look nice. I need to look like you, but authoritative so they take me seriously."

Rowan tugged on my hand, pulling me away from my frantic clothing shuffle. When I tried to release him, he pulled me close and trapped me in the circle of his arms. "Hey." He tilted my chin up with his index finger. "No matter what you wear, they'll all take you seriously because you'll be the biggest predator in the room."

I snorted. "Sure." I tried to pull away again, but Rowan wouldn't let me go.

"Evie."

I huffed and stilled. "We're going to be late."

His lips twitched. "They will wait. The meeting is about us, after all."

"Yes, but I don't want them making any major decisions without us."

"Do you always worry this much?"

My eyes narrowed. Rowan made it difficult to be cranky. "Yes."

He grinned. "You made me the largest territory owner in the U.S., and they can't take the land back, can they?"

I lifted a shoulder in a shrug. "They can try, but now that I'm keeping a closer eye on things, they won't be successful."

"Then we have nothing to worry about."

"The Lords don't seem like the kind of crowd who'll let something like this stand."

He lowered his voice and bent to touch his forehead to mine. "Then we'll teach them why it's a good idea to learn a new skill." The words are low and deadly, his self-confidence over this dangerous gambit making something tug deep inside me.

Rowan had a deep sense of self-possession I found profoundly sexy. Caelan was always in your face, prone to violent outbursts of rage. The man had destroyed my shop over the automaton I'd made when he forced me to work for him. Standing here now, I could never picture Rowan doing something like that. A certainty clanged in my head like a gong.

Rowan would never hurt me.

"I can almost hear the gears in your brain turning," he murmured.

"I'm wondering why I made the decisions I've made."

His smile was sad. "We've all made decisions we've come to regret later. The only thing you can do is learn from them for the future."

"I'm scared," I admitted. "Not of the Lords necessarily, but of what might happen today. Every time I have to deal with them, I become regrettably angry."

Rowan's laugh soothed something inside me. "They're skilled at getting under everyone's skin. I must have missed that day in class when they were handing out Lord lessons. Remember you are no longer under their authority."

"I'm under yours."

Rowan shook his head. "You are the queen of the fae and under no one's authority. You live in my territory because you've chosen to." He brushed my hair away from my face. "Never doubt your power, Evie. The Lords are merely shifters. Powerful ones, no doubt, but shifters all the same. If they wish to play dangerous games, show them why those games are a bad idea."

I put my hand over his. "You always say such wonderful things to me."

Rowan said nothing but brought me in for a tight hug. "It's far too cold for a dress." He let go and flipped through my clothing with a critical eye, setting a few pieces aside. "Warm slacks and a sweater. Blue or green will bring out the color of your eyes. Minimal jewelry. Wear boots you can run in." He winked and stepped back. "Just in case."

"I'll be out in less than ten."

Rowan stepped out of the bedroom. "I'll make a pot of coffee."

THE LORD HAD A GOOD EYE. I dressed in a pair of brown slacks and a maroon crew neck cashmere sweater with a pair of comfortable, heeled brown boots. I added a leopard-print belt with a gold buckle. To keep with the minimal but stylish look, I added a pair of gold hoops and a gold necklace with a London Topaz drop.

There wasn't enough time to curl my hair, so I wove a quick fishtail braid, securing the bulk with an elastic tie I found in the toiletry bag Dad had left me. Rowan was waiting for me in the living room, testing out my new couch.

He nodded when he saw me. "You look nice. No one who sees you today will assume you could take out the entire room with a snap of your fingers."

My lips twisted. "A snap is probably an exaggeration, but being underestimated is one of my favorite things."

We grinned at each other. Rowan handed me a travel mug of coffee and a small black box he took from his pocket. I hesitated and met his eyes.

"A small token, a secret between us. No one else will know what it means, but it would honor me if you wore it today."

I set the mug down and snapped the box open. A gold necklace rested within the velvet, but that wasn't what made me gasp.

Hanging on the end was a carved golden owl, its eyes two small rose-cut rubies. "Rowan," I breathed. "This is stunning." My fingers brushed over the delicate wings. "We haven't had much time to speak about your fae form."

I glanced up to see him watching me, his irises outlined in gold. "You know my mother is a shapeshifter."

I nodded.

"The owl was one of her favorite forms when I was a child. She preferred the horned owl, but mine was always a snowy owl." A soft smile hovered over his mouth. "I don't see her much these days, not since…"

I needed to check with Mom and Dad to see if anything had come from my request. "I'm sorry. I'll fix that, I swear to you."

He gave a sharp shake of his head. "Not your fault."

Untrue, but he kept speaking. "I've never shared that secret with anyone else. It helps knowing someone who is a little like me shares a small part of me."

I wanted to say I couldn't accept such an elaborate and expensive gift, but there was so much hope and a tender vulnerability on his face, that I swallowed hard and nodded. "I'd be honored," I said in a hoarse voice.

Rowan stood. I handed him the box and turned, sweeping my braid over my shoulder. While he was removing the owl necklace, I unfastened the topaz pendant and set it on the coffee table.

Rowan settled the pendant around my neck. His warm fingers swept across the back of my neck as he fastened the new one. When he finished, I adjusted the pendant and turned.

Rowan's eyes glittered with warmth.

"I love it," I said quietly. "Thank you for trusting me with something so precious."

A knock on the door interrupted. Rowan stepped away. "Ready to go? I secured us a ride."

I snatched my purse from the hallway table and checked inside to make sure I had everything I needed. "Ready if you are."

Rowan opened the door. My father stood on the steps, his eyes swirling with magic. I kissed Dad on the cheek and waited for Rowan.

"I'll be close by if things go sideways," Dad said. "Hold on to me and don't let go until we've arrived."

A moment later, we were traveling through space and time.

I hated bringing her to this viper den, but it was hard to miss the stunning figure Evie cut as she sailed through the lobby doors wearing my mark. Cernunnos stood beside me as we watched, but as I made to follow, he spoke.

"A moment."

I waited, annoyed he was keeping me from her. The other Lords offered deference to Cernunnos, and I did as well, but I was decidedly less meek than the others while in his presence. My mother, as the god well knew, could give him a run for his money, and she would be less than pleased if Cernunnos acted against me.

Evie and I hadn't had much of a chance to talk about what my heritage could mean for the future, but we would. Soon.

"You haven't finalized the bond."

"I won't until she's ready. If she ever is." Not that I had much choice the second time when the bond had snapped into place far more firmly than the first time. To think of the possibility of Evie never accepting the bond between us caused unfathomable pain, but I would never force her to do something she wasn't ready for. I was not Caelan and would never be him. She was still too heartsore to fully understand the ramifications of what such a thing meant to both of us.

"She claimed your land, though."

"With my blessing." I stared after Evie, still stalking through the lobby. "Her magic is a wonder."

"There is far more at play here than a simple spell. I suspect the gods are at their games again. Evie is still coming into her power and will need someone strong by her side."

"She has someone." I grew tired of these political machinations long ago. If I could shed the trappings of the Lordship, I would have, but if I wasn't in power, someone worse would take my place and lead my people into ruin.

"Even if she never gives you what you most desire?"

My fists clenched at my sides. "You know nothing about me. Having Evie in my life has been an honor, and every moment I spend with her is one I will cherish. The man you're looking for is Caelan. Speak to him if you're looking for the man who sought to use her for what she could give him."

Cernunnos chuckled. "Be wary of the other Lord in there. Caelan has been in a rage since Evie left him."

I stared at him. He was not telling me anything I didn't already know. So why was he delaying me? What did he really want?

Seeing my suspicion, Cernunnos sighed. "I love my daughter and only wish to see her happy. But there are duties she must fulfill. Ensure you do not get in the way."

I'd never thought of striking a god until that moment. How dare he assume I would ever stand in Evie's way? Cernunnos, seeming to realize my current state of mind, disappeared in a gust of wind.

"Asshole," I muttered. Getting my mental state back to a normal state took a moment, but once I'd collected myself, I smoothed down my sweater and followed Evie inside.

She sat at a table in the hotel lobby, a pink drink sitting before her. "I ordered you an Old Fashioned. Hope that's okay."

"A fortifying drink is always in order before facing the firing squad."

Her laugh warmed my heart. The server dropped off the drink and hurried away without a word. This hotel was well used to odd things occurring when we all convened and had gotten good at ignoring everything, especially when we tipped well.

"This sucks," Evie said quietly.

I picked up my drink and took a sip. Top-shelf whiskey and a hint of cherry. Evie smiled. "I guessed. Hope I got it right."

"It's perfect." And it was. Even if she'd gotten it wrong, she'd thought of me and that would always be enough.

"Have you ever thought of disbanding the Lords?" She'd dropped her voice almost to a whisper.

I sat back and studied her. "Every time I have to meet with them," I said honestly.

Evie blinked in surprise. "Seriously?"

"Of course. Not all of them are bad. Maybe none of them are. But absolute power does no one any good. Thorvin and I are the only Lords who've never made a play for another one's territory. Perhaps your Ben will be added into that equation soon enough."

Evie blushed. "He's not my Ben."

My fingertips played over the top of the crystal glass. "He wants to be." She had history with the large Healer. If he would have played his cards right, she and I wouldn't be sitting here right now. I'd never been so glad of the idiocy of men as I was right now.

Evie sipped her ridiculous drink. "He'd never accept me as I am. I haven't seen or heard from anyone since the incident in Joy Springs, so all the allies I thought I might have gathered dried up like raisins in the sun."

I can feel her disappointment in the spot in my chest where she resides. The incomplete bond. She's not all the way there yet, but when her emotions are strong, I can feel the wildness of her inside my heart.

"He might have wanted something more before then, but now I'm sure he'd rather be as far away from me as possible."

There's a tang of bitterness in her voice I hated to hear. She'd always been at odds with the beast inside her, but now that the paranormal world knows what she is, she expected everyone to turn on her. Perhaps they had.

"Those who shun you now aren't worthy of your presence or your protection. Let them rot for all I care."

She peered at me, a strange look on her face. "Do all of your people know what I am?"

I told them moments before I arrived in Joy Springs to take her back with me. "They do."

"None of them are worried about me being there?"

"They trust in me enough to know I would never lead them astray or introduce a danger I could not control. But you have never been a danger to me or my people. Not even when you felt you could not control yourself. You are far too conscientious, even when drowning in magic. But, when we return, I believe you should invite Barrett to the Keep. There is much he can still teach you."

"Did he call you?" Evie grumbled.

"He did. I can't help but agree with him. He's helped you when you needed someone. Now is your chance to help him, and those like you."

A young man dressed in a suit came to our table. "The Lords are ready." He dipped his head and hurried away.

I tossed the rest of my drink back. "Are you ready?"

Evie grimaced. "Ready as I'll ever be."

Together, we rose and walked to the Lords' den.

CHAPTER
Thirty-Two

Hate pulsed from Caelan. I felt it slither over my skin and settle into the spot over my heart where the bond lay. His golden gaze flicked over me, disgust etched onto his face before his attention slid to Rowan who stood beside me, his hand a comforting weight against the small of my back.

Ethan's eyebrows rose when he saw us standing together. A moment later, his nostrils flared, and his attention snapped to Caelan, his eyes wary.

Ben stared at me, a thoughtful look on his face. He didn't seem scared or wary or anything. More contemplative than anything.

Soren wore a smirk of amusement. "My, my, my," he drawled. "I'm usually excellent at chess, but even I never saw this checkmate coming." He slid a sly look Caelan's way. "Incomplete, Lord. Maybe you still have a chance."

Ben sighed. "Soren. Can you shut the fuck up for once in your life?"

Soren winked at me. "Never, Healer. My witty verbal repartee is the only thing keeping me alive."

Dario, who had not yet been appointed as Lord to my knowledge, sat at the table watching the exchange like a tennis match.

When our eyes met, fury made his nostrils flare. The wannabe Lord had hazel eyes, like Rowan, but his held more green in the iris, along with chips of amber color swimming in the depths. Like all the Lords, he was pretty, but there was a shallowness to his character I didn't like. It didn't help that he looked like he walked off the set of a local television vampire drama series.

Dario was fuming that I'd ripped the territory away from him, not caring that it wasn't his to start with.

"Please," Thorvin said, rising from the long table. "Have a seat." He pointed to two chairs facing the Lords' table.

It was then I noticed the table the Lords were sitting at had no room for Rowan. They'd made him an outsider. And I knew at that moment, this was all my fault.

Rowan's gaze took in the chairs and the table. A wicked chuckle rumbled his chest. "So it has come to this."

Thorvin sighed. I liked the Lord, and though I found his slightly harried and harassed countenance amusing, I knew, just like the others, he was not someone to take at face value. He'd proven himself deadly enough when Moira, Garrett, and I had trespassed on his land.

"Rowan, you've expanded far beyond the boundaries of your agreed-to territory." Thorvin sat back down and rubbed his temples.

"So?" he asked.

Caelan snorted. "You think just because Evie is an ally now that you can take our land from us?"

"Your land was taken by might," I interjected. "Won by skill and taken by power, the land is mine to do with as I see fit."

"And you believe Rowan is fit?" Caelan said, his eyes burning molten gold.

Fury burned in my chest, and I reveled in my rage. "More than others," I said, knowing how much the words would infuriate him.

Soren chuckled. "Evie, darling, you do know how to keep a bonfire burning long after it has turned to embers, don't you?"

Claws slid from Caelan's fingers, his jaw tightening. "Be careful who you speak to," he warned.

"You should take the same advice," I snapped. "All of you. Dario is not a Lord and not entitled to the territory. Even if you did make him a Lord, I've already proven I can strip the land from one if I need to."

"Are you threatening us?" Ethan asked. His tone wasn't angry for once. He watched me with a healthy new respect, a look I was not used to seeing from him.

"I'm telling you to let sleeping dogs lie. I shared the land with Rowan because he is a good and decent Lord, and our powers complement each other. He has no designs on encroaching on anyone else's territory."

Rowan slid a look my way, one that heated my blood. "Which is another reason we are here," he said. "A darkness creeps among our lands, driven by what we think are the gods. It begins as a dark poison, killing everything it touches, until it affects the Lord who walks the land. We are here to ask you to allow Evie to come onto your lands and purge the poison. She will need to temporarily claim the borders until the magic is completely purged."

Caelan burst out laughing. "She's already tried that once. Absolutely not. Evie is not here on a goodwill mission. Donovan's lands have already fallen to her. She seeks to claim more until the Lords are no more."

"I could have left that darkness rotting inside your body," I snapped. "Instead, it continues poisoning your lands until it will eventually claim you, your land, and your people."

Rowan tugged me into the seat next to him and wove our fingers together. Caelan's lips curled with disgust when he noticed. His touch brought me back to reality, sending the anger deep inside. "Have any of you started feeling poorly over the last few weeks? Fatigue, weakness, dizziness, or emotional outbursts?"

No one admitted to anything, but Soren's eyes narrowed. He

studied me with intensity, and I can almost see the wheels turning in his mind.

"That's what the magic does. I do not know its purpose yet. Moira has a certain talent, and she's using her powers to help us track down the magic source. Once we find it, we will know more on how to control it and destroy it for good. My magic has proven successful against it, as your Lord—" I inclined my head toward Caelan, "will attest to."

"Provided he's not being a little bitch," Rowan said, showing his teeth to the other Lord.

Soren choked on a laugh.

Caelan said nothing, color touching high on his cheeks.

"Caelan?" Ethan asked. "Is she telling the truth?"

For a moment, I thought he would lie, but after a long moment, Caelan gives a begrudging nod. "She trespassed on my territory, told me of this spell, and forced a healing on me."

Soren's eyebrows flicked up. "Good gracious, man. You're so hardheaded you'd turn down a healing from the godsdamned Fae Queen?"

Caelan ignored Soren, but the others stared hard at him, making me wonder what they were thinking. Was this the first sign of a fracture between them?

"Up until a few days ago, she was your fiancée, man," Thorvin said. "If you cannot trust her, who can you trust?"

"You know what she is," Caelan said.

Soren chortled. "You'd have to live under a rock not to. The woman hasn't harmed any of us unless we came after her first. Even Ethan, the hardheaded sonofabastard he is, acknowledged this."

Ethan sent him an annoyed look. "Yes, I am aware I've been a—"

"A right bastard," Soren cheerfully supplied. "And rightfully deserved getting tossed around like a rag doll."

Rowan chuckled under his breath.

"We are duty-sworn to kill Chimeras," Caelan growled.

I jerk back in alarm. Rowan squeezed my hand.

"Then you should have killed her long ago," he said. "Because you've known longer than any of us what she is. So you are just as complicit, aren't you?"

Caelan doesn't like being confronted with the truth. "It's amusing to see how much of an ally you've become to our resident Chimera now that your head has been between her legs."

A shocked gasp escaped me. "Caelan," I breathed in horror.

To my surprise, Rowan doesn't outwardly react. That spot in my chest flared with heat, lending me insight into his internal fury, but instead, Rowan smiled. "You lash out at others when your judgment is questioned, deflection of the highest order. I told you once before, Lord, insult Evie again at your own peril."

Ethan stood, holding out his hands. "Please. We are supposed to be above petty fights."

Rowan slid his furious gaze to the Lord. "Insulting my mate is not petty, Ethan. We both know how you'd react if someone spoke against yours, so don't question me when I defend mine."

The word mate sparks heat inside me. I wasn't his official mate, but there was enough of a bond to spark his territorial instinct. Even before, he would have defended me. Now, I suspect he would die for me.

Soren slid Caelan a disgusted glance. "What the fuck is wrong with you? You've lost. Everyone sitting here knows this woman gave you multiple chances to get your head out of your ass, and you managed to fail every single time. You can't blame Rowan for picking up the pieces, especially if he knew this entire time what she was to him and still let her decide." His head shake is disgusted, but his words made my attention snap to Rowan, a question burning in my eyes.

His thumb stroked the back of my hand. "Later," he murmured.

"This is not what we should be discussing," Ethan interjected. After a quelling look at Caelan, he turned to me. "Tell us what you know about this magic."

At Rowan's dark look, Ethan cleared his throat. "Please."

"There isn't much to tell. Right now, it doesn't seem to have a specific target. The magic kills what it touches or slowly poisons what it can't kill right away. Moira and my father are working together to determine its source."

Soren jerked upright. "Moira is working with Cernunnos?"

"She is."

"For how long?" He wipes his face of emotion.

"For however long it takes, I suppose."

Rowan snorted. "The vampire is living in my territory. We can arrange a visit if Moira allows one."

"She won't," Soren grumbled.

Ethan waved a hand. "You claim to be able to purge this magic. How are we to trust you won't wrest our territories from us?"

"Trust is built on a foundation of faith. I've never had a lust for power, nor have I gone after anyone who didn't come after me first. You will have to take me at my word."

Caelan's disgusted snort sounded like a gunshot.

I turned blazing eyes to him and stood. "Your derision is well noted but undeserved, Lord. You can rot on your property for all I care anymore. You've had your chance to accept my help, and I will not offer assistance again. Perhaps when your land is dead due to your neglect, I will come in to claim the territory." The Chimera showed through my eyes. "If you continue to speak down to me, I will show you exactly what I am made of."

Caelan, never one to back down, rose from his seat. "You've been nothing but a disappointment to me."

Rowan started to rise, but I put a hand on his shoulder. I could take care of this myself.

"I learned from the best," I said with a smile.

Soren watched us carefully, his muscles tensed to move if we exploded.

Caelan's laugh is sharp and cutting. "I vote to strip Rowan of his Lordship."

"Thank the gods," Rowan said.

A surprised laugh bubbled from my throat. I glanced at him. He's handsome and mussed and wearing an exasperated expression. "They can't have the land even if they strip me of power. My family owns all 1,500 acres."

Ethan's eyes widened. Ben, who's remained silent the entire time, bursts out laughing. Thorvin rubbed his hands over his face, and Soren grinned like the Cheshire cat.

Caelan looked like he was about to explode.

"No one knew?" I asked him.

"Nope." To the others, he spread his hands out. "Please do it but know my people will rebel against anyone else you try to assign. You will not be allowed to reside anywhere on my property. Good luck being a Lord for a land you can't enter."

Ethan sighed and sat back down. "You won't get off so easily, Rowan. We have no intention of stripping your titles away." Then he looked at Caelan. "Your outbursts grow tiring. Evie has made some good points. If what she says is true, we are all in danger."

"I'm not," Rowan gloated.

"Keep rubbing it in," Soren grumbled.

"Dario has the right to challenge you for the territory," Caelan said to Rowan.

I rolled my eyes. "He has the right to challenge us both. The territory belongs to us both."

Dario glanced at me. I smile and let a bit of the Chimera roll over my irises.

The wannabe Lord blanched and threw his hands up. "Yeah. I'm out." Dario shoved his chair from behind and stalked out the door, muttering something to himself in Spanish that sounded vaguely like "*un montón de hijos de puta locos.*"

I didn't know Spanish, but I was positive the words meant something like, "these people are too well-adjusted and normal for me to ever fit in here."

No one said a word for a long moment after the door slammed. Ethan was the first to break. His long-suffering sigh almost made me laugh. The Lord sagged against his seat and muttered, "I owe you an apology."

I blinked. Was I hallucinating? Why were the Lords being so reasonable today?

Ethan drew a long breath. "Things were as normal as they could be until we got involved in your life. We should have stayed out of things." He shot a dark look at Caelan. "*All* of us. Everything that happened afterward was the result of our meddling, and that led to both unforeseen and unfortunate consequences." Our eyes met. "We threatened you and violated your privacy and brought our wrath down upon your head, and as such broke our own rules about staying out of a private citizen's life."

The other Lords watched him, surprise on their faces. Though Caelan still looked pissed off, which seemed his usual state these days.

"Though we do not know each other well, I now believe everything you did was caused by what we did to you first, and for that you have my sincere apology, for I spearheaded much of the antagonistic attitude toward you."

"Are you alright?" I blurted.

Ethan snorted and rubbed his eyes. "I am tired of fighting, of this strife, of alienating people for no godsdamned reason. And now you are mated to one of our own. Or close to it. Our behavior has been egregious, but now, if everything you say is true, we require your help. You are well within your rights to deny us, though your presence and offer is a good show of faith since we all know you could easily strip our lands from us if you truly wanted. Not all of us are young. Some of us remember your ancestors and their claim on this world. We know who could hold our chains once more if we keep going the way we have been. I have treated you the worst, and all I can do now is apologize and tell you I will do my best to change my ways. I am not your enemy, nor do I want to be. I ask that you allow us to cast our vote to accept or deny your help, in private, and, in return, you allow this autonomy and do not try to take our property by force."

I stared at him, stunned by his words, never expecting this mea culpa from Ethan of all people. Silence drew out. Caelan's rage was palpable. Soren seems unaffected. Ben and Thorvin looked at Ethan with new respect. And Rowan seemed stoic, but I could feel a hint of the chaos of his emotions through our link.

There's only one thing I could say. "Very well." I rose and walked to the door. To my surprise, Rowan followed.

"I already voted." He winked and held the door open for me.

We walked back to the lobby bar and reclaimed our table. "Do you think he'll stab us in the back?" I blurted.

Rowan's face is contemplative. "No. Ethan is an asshole a lot of the time, but he is a man of his word." He scrubbed a hand over his cheek and chuckled. "I'm surprised by this turn of events. I thought things would go much worse."

"Me too," I admitted.

We ordered another drink and made small talk for a while, but I'm distracted by Ethan's words. He was right, but everything that happened led me first to Caelan and then to Rowan. How could I ever be sorry for that? I found my father and was rebuilding bonds with my mother and had a new place to live. I'd discovered unfathomable things about my power and had taken the fae crown. My life had done a complete one-eighty. Not all the changes were good, but no one, not even the fae, lived in a perfect world.

The same young man from before came over and announced the Lords were ready for us once more.

The air was decidedly more hostile when we entered for the second time. If Caelan could kill us with a glare he would have.

We retook our seats. Ethan steepled his fingertips and opened his mouth to speak.

The door flew open and slammed against the wall, the loud crack of wood shattering the silence. Moira stumbled in. Her hair was in wild disarray around her head and her dark eyes wide with horror.

"Joy Springs," she croaked. "The magic is—"

A banshee scream sent us all to the floor. Shouts of alarm rang through the room, but not a single shifter could rise against Tess. The banshee floated in, pale hair floating around her head in a haunting corona of silver light. Her mouth was open wide, an empty cavern of darkness and sound, her scream reverberating through our bones.

Tess's eyes glowed an unearthly silver as they swept over me and Rowan, her scream fading into a soft echo. My shoulders sagged with relief. Her eyes fell on Ethan, then Soren…

My heart stuttered with terror.

"No," I breathed.

She bypassed Thorvin, then Ben, and slowly lifted a pale hand and pointed at Caelan.

"Marked," Tess moaned. "You are marked for death."

CHAPTER
Thirty~Three

Tess collapsed. Chaos reigned in the room. Moira scooped the banshee up and rushed over to me, grabbing me by the elbow.

"We have to go." Her voice was low and urgent.

"We can't let Caelan die," I snapped.

"I don't give a shit about Caelan. I care about you." She looked at Rowan. "Help me."

Rowan looked torn but slowly shook his head. "I won't force Evie to come with us." He looked at me. "What do you wish to do?"

Another piece of the stone surrounding my heart broke off. I touched his chest, then turned to hurry to Caelan still lying on the ground.

Like the others, he was having trouble shaking off the effects of Tess's scream. He pressed a hand to his head and groaned.

I touched his elbow. "Caelan. You need to come with us. Now."

He jerked away. "I'm not going anywhere with you."

I bit down my scream of frustration. "A banshee is never wrong. You will die if you don't allow me to help you."

His brow furrowed. "There's no one here."

"Tess is down for the count and won't wake up for a while. I have no information. If you return to your land, you very well might die. I can hide you in the fae lands for a little while until we figure out what's going on."

His storm eyes flashed with gold. "How do I know this isn't some ploy to take my lands?"

Rowan swore under his breath. "For god's sake man. I need to get you a tinfoil hat to wear because all you spout is conspiracy these days."

I let out a slow breath and tried one more time to reason with him. "Caelan, at one time, you trusted me with your life. I'm asking you to trust me now. I don't know when or where death is going to come for you, but it will come. Please. Let me help you."

Once upon a time, Caelan would have taken my hand and gone with me. He would have trusted me, and we would have won every battle we fought together. But now, with Rowan by my side, with that bond growing stronger every day, he looked at me with distrust and more than a little bit of disgust.

"Caelan," I begged, tears thick in my throat. "Please. No matter what happened between us, I never wanted this for you. I swear to you I will help."

But Caelan pushed himself up from the floor and stood.

Ethan came over. "Caelan. A banshee's scream is never wrong. Let her help."

Caelan's look of betrayal would live forever in my nightmares. "I do not need her help. Evie means nothing to me. She made her choices, as did I, and now we will both live with them, come what may."

Ethan stared at Caelan and slowly shook his head. Ben came up. "Caelan, perhaps you should—"

Caelan bared his teeth and shoved his way through the two Lords. Soren came up and watched him go. "Idiot," he said sadly. "I'll miss the crabby sonofabitch."

Ben choked out a laugh. "You dark bastard."

Soren grinned unrepentantly. "If anyone will find a way out, it will be that slippery prick."

As Caelan's broad back disappeared around the corner, I could only hope Soren was right.

Not long after, all of us gathered around Rowan's kitchen table. Declan and Hope stood together by the counter munching on cheese and crackers. I was too wound up to eat anything, and Rowan was pacing back and forth, his face a mask of concentration.

I felt awful. No matter what I felt for Caelan, I didn't want him to die. I didn't want any of the Lords to die, but Caelan and I had been through so much together. Being self-aware was a curse because I knew we'd never have the relationship we once did, nor did I want one, but our camaraderie was shattered too. I doubted we'd ever be able to sit in a room together without being antagonistic toward each other.

None of it mattered. Caelan was marked for death. Banshees never lied.

And speaking of the banshee, she also sat at the table, her pale countenance even whiter than normal. Tess had little information, only a vague notion of a timeline.

Within a few weeks was all she'd say. She didn't know where the threat came from, when it would strike, or how it would happen.

We'd gone through a few plans, but all of it revolved around Caelan's cooperation, and we all knew he would not give it if I was involved.

I could take his land by force and take him against his will, but doing so would shatter him. Taking his choice away would break something inside me, and I refused to consider the option.

A few hours later, everyone but Rowan had gone their own way, leaving us in a quiet kitchen.

He sat down beside me.

"I'm sorry," I said.

Rowan put his hand over mine. "You loved him, may still love him. Caelan is a lucky man to have someone love him so fiercely."

I swallowed hard, the truth forcing its way through my lips. "I don't love him anymore. Not like that. Too much has happened. His hatred for what I represent broke us. I—I can't love someone like that. Maybe I never loved him like he needed. I don't know. But letting him die…" I shook my head. "I can't do it, Rowan. No matter what he's done."

"Then we will save him," he said simply.

His words crack another piece of stone from my heart, and another, and another. As my barriers fell against his goodness, I rose from my chair and straddled his lap, my hands cupping his face. "Give me time," I whispered.

His hands buried themselves in my hair, and I leaned forward, my lips brushing over his. I place one of my hands over his heart and feel the strong, steady beat. How could I have missed this? Was I so blind to not see how he felt about me every time he looked at me, every time he held a hand out when I stumbled? A tear snaked down my face.

Rowan reached up and brushed it away. My body trembled at his touch.

"You shall have all the time you need," he responded.

Epilogue

THE MOTHER, THE MAIDEN, & THE CRONE

"Stop this madness," Cliona snapped. "You would poison the world to see your goals realized?"

"I would do much worse," the ancient goddess responded. "Don't act so high and mighty. We all know what you did for your daughter. How is this any different?"

Cliona stared in horror. "I did not kill anyone. Protecting my daughter is what a mother should do. You poison their world to prove a point!"

"I poison their world to let them know who really rules, Banshee Queen. If they decide not to listen, their deaths will be on their heads."

"Mortals and Lords do not play the games of gods," said the younger goddess who lounged on a chaise lounge made of pure gold. "They're too stupid to realize this is a lesson. They'll mobilize and stand against us."

The ancient goddess let out a snort of derision. "And they will lose once more."

But Cliona's eyes narrowed. "Are you truly foolish enough to think my daughter would stand with gods who indiscriminately murder her people?"

"We are her people!" the ancient one roared. "This is your fault, Cliona. You coddled her and allowed humans to raise her instead of bringing her up to realize her full power."

The younger goddess slid her golden legs off the lounge and sat up. She slid a wary glance toward the ancient crone. "Times are different. Perhaps we should find a way to work together instead of—"

"SILENCE!" the ancient one thundered.

Cliona was not so easily deterred. "You can stop this at any time. Withdraw your power."

"It's not my power," the crone chortled. "A witch helps me, keeping the spell going through the blood I send her."

Cliona shook her head. "You give your power away with no heed to the danger it will bring down around our heads. I think, sister, you will find Evie not so easily swayed to your cause. If you harm anyone she cares about, she will rise up and become the force none of us are ready to deal with."

The ancient one was too far gone in her ideals to listen to the warning. Her rheumy eyes lit up. "Embracing her power is her destiny. She will be the ruler we all need and take our lands back from those who've stolen them!"

The younger goddess edged away from the crone.

Cliona stepped back, away from the poisonous goddess who might bring ruin to their people. "I will stand with my daughter no matter which way she decides to go."

The ancient crone gasped at Cliona's perceived betrayal and lifted a gnarled, crooked finger at the goddess. "Then you too shall perish at my hand."

Cliona's smile is a terrible thing to behold. "You underestimate my daughter. I look forward to the day when she rises and shows you exactly who she is meant to be."

The ancient lunged for the queen, but Cliona had known for years how treacherous her many sisters were. With a laugh like bells, the Banshee Queen disappeared into a mist of power, there and gone in an instant, leaving the vengeful goddess and her meek and wavering accomplice behind.

———

Keep reading for a look at Book Eight
Goddess Shifting

Goddess Shifting

BOOK 8, SHIFTER LORDS

When you strike a deal with the fae, make sure you read all the fine print…

After nearly draining herself to save Rowan, Evie has called off all training to get some much-needed rest. Once again, the universe has a field day with her plans.
Evie thought she was the last living female Chimera.
She's wrong.

When a baby is dropped off at the shop, Evie has no idea how to react. As she searches for the parents, it quickly becomes evident the child is no human or fae. She's full-blooded Chimera, meaning there are at least two others out there like her.

But why would they give her their baby? And why is Evie thinking about keeping her?

Talk about throwing a wrench into her already complicated life.

As Evie and her friends search to uncover the mystery surrounding the child, other forces swirl around them, attempting to unbalance Evie and derail everything she's worked so hard for.

Once again, everything is changing, but Evie finally knows who and what she wants.

It's time for a fae bargain, one Evie hopes will finally bring her into her destiny.

Will it be a happy ever after, or is this just the start of Evie's final downfall?

Trailer Park Transylvania

Psychic Cleaner

The Magical Soapmaker Mysteries

The Goddess Chronicles

Vikings of Virginia

The Deadicated Matchmaker

About the Author

Sheryl likes cake too much and can be found hoarding it while hiding from her children in the pantry closet.

Follow her on Amazon at: https://www.amazon.com/S-E-Babin/e/B00J1J236A

A small press bound by the belief that every voice matters.

Sign up for our newsletter to learn about new releases and more.
https://oliver-heberbooks.com/subscribe/

Follow us on social media:

facebook.com/oliverheberbooks
instagram.com/oliverheberbooks
amazon.com/oliverheberbooks
youtube.com/@OliverHeberBooksPublisher